Also by
From Indigo Sea Press

A New Beginning

Love Finds a Way

indigoseapress.com

The Box in the Attic

By

Joan Byrd

Deep Indigo Books
Published by Indigo Sea Press
Winston-Salem

Deep Indigo Books
Indigo Sea Press
PO Box 67201
Winston-Salem, NC 27114
This book is a work of fiction. Names, characters, locations and events are either a product of the author's imagination, fictitious or used fictitiously. Any resemblance to any event, locale or person, living or dead, is purely coincidental.

First Deep Indigo Books edition published
August, 2018
Deep Indigo Books, Moon Sailor and all production design are trademarks of Indigo Sea Press, used under license.

For information regarding bulk purchases of this book, digital purchase and special discounts, please contact the publisher at indigoseapress@gmail.com

Cover Concept by Joan Byrd
Cover design by Pan Morelli
Manufactured in the United States of America
ISBN 978-1-63066-486-2

I grew up on a farm just like Hattie,

with a loving family like the Russels,

so I dedicate this book to them:

My Mama & Daddy: Tip & Dot Bodsford

who live in heaven with our Lord

and my five beautiful sisters:

Barbara Smith, Carolyn Joyner, Janice Foster,

Linda Nasser and Yvonne Ketner.

As always: Ray, my loving husband,

Patrick, my angelic storyteller

and my greatest thanks goes to our Holy Family,

God the Father, the Son, Jesus Christ,

and the Holy Spirit.

Without them there would be

no story to tell.

Chapter 1

What strange unsolved mystery lies in the walls of the once majestic old mansion that sits quietly overlooking the small old town of Sleepy Creek. It's once stately rooms, now covered in years of decay and dust, reflect only a small glimpse into the family that had been long forgotten by the town's people.

Nothing inside had been changed since their mysterious disappearance nearly two hundred years ago. Despite the age of the old house, it was in remarkable shape, missing only a few shingles here and there.

During the daylight hours, the old house looked weather beaten, due to having never been painted. The dark shutters hung closed, as they had been for decades. Despite the attempts from the town council to tear down the old mansion, the last living relative refused and ordered everyone to stay off his property.

William Franklin Marshall had been named after the original owner of the Marshall mansion and was the town's biggest employer. He had started the Marshall Mill, which was still in operation and owned by the cranky William F. Marshall.

Although Mr. Marshall appeared to be in his early forties, he acted much older to those who had a chance meeting with the old standoff recluse. Although he refused to have the mansion torn down, he never set foot in the place. He chose to live at the far side of town in a small stone house, dating back as old as the old mansion itself. According to the legends passed down from one generation to the next, the first William Marshall was a very friendly, happy, family man.

The story went that William Marshall and his wife Susanne had moved to the once rundown town of Sleepy Creek and fell in love with the place. Mr. Marshall had a vision of what the town could become and with his help, he would bring it alive. They purchased up most of the land surrounding Sleepy Creek, including the bluff overlooking it. The marvelous mansion was built and Sleepy Creek began to grow. The mill made a place for employment and the shops grew into quaint businesses, such as the Sleepy Creek Bakery and

Café, Micky's Grocery Store and Hardware, Libby's Library, stocked with the old classics, a small school, the popular Christmas Attic and everyone's favorite, Mrs. Nettie's Cookie factory, known for her sugar and molasses cookies.

The Marshall's had one daughter, according to the stories passed down. She too made friends easily at school and in the small Methodist church that set right in the middle of town. Its tall steeple could be seen for miles, as it was the only tall building on town square.

The friendly family started the Christmas Holiday Jolly Getaway, and put Sleepy Creek on the map for tourist to make their small town their Christmas tradition. Even two hundred years later, the Christmas spectacular the town puts on, brings in hundreds of people, from Thanksgiving, straight through to New Year.

During the daytime, the town is alive with lots of activities, but when night falls on Sleepy Creek, everyone stays within their home. What are they afraid of? Could it be the things they've been told about the sad old mansion. The darkness drops over the tall ghostly house as if something inside needed to be hidden and yet few people had been brave enough to go see for themselves the strange glow that appears in the attic.

So, it sits there in the shadows of the old oak trees, that are overgrown with vines and moss. The old house sits there, high on the hill, all alone…or is it?

Just on the outskirts of town, live the fifth generation of the Russel family. The old farm has been in operation ever since the first Russel came to Sleepy Creek, around the same time as the Marshall family. The Russel's were among most of the families living in the small town, each taking up were their past relative vacated, mostly in the Methodist cemetery, nestled behind the church in a grove of pine trees.

Nettie and Gideon Russel, along with their son, Adam, and his wife Carolyn, live and work on the farm now. Adam and Carolyn are keeping the Russel name alive by having a house full of Russel children, eight boys and one girl, the youngest, Hattie, age ten. The eight boys are a big help on the farm and at the cookie factory, named after their grandmother Nettie. They range in age of thirteen to twenty, starting with the oldest, Andrew, age twenty. Then there's

The Box in the Attic

Peter, nineteen, Philip, eighteen, James, seventeen, John, sixteen, Matthew, fifteen, Simon, fourteen, and Thomas, age thirteen.

Grandpa Gideon insisted naming everyone born a Russel to be given a name from the bible, so Adam and Carolyn chose from Jesus' disciples to name their eight sons. So, ten- year- old Hattie didn't understand why they chose not to name her from a bible ancestor. Was she not a Russel like her eight brothers or was the fact that she was born a girl?

Hattie sat pondering this for the millionth time as she sat at the kitchen table, her elbows pressed firmly on the starched white tablecloth, her face resting in her palms. Hattie was drawn away from her thought when her grandmother opened the old white oven door and pulled the Thanksgiving turkey out to base for the fourth time. Hattie closed her eyes in delight as she stiffed the air. Never had she smelled a better bird, well, maybe last Thanksgiving, but that seem like ages ago to the young ten-year-old.

The sound of the oven door closing made Hattie sat up and watch her grandma sit down to cut up potatoes for her famous mash potatoes. As Nettie Russel peeled each potato, Hattie watched, ready with lots of questions, which she was often inspired to do.

"Grandma, Jane Tanner said their bed and breakfast was completely filled up for the Christmas Holly Jolly Getaway! Amy Collins said her parents had to order more Christmas items for the Christmas Attic. And it just Thanksgiving! Do you think there are more visitors coming this year to Sleepy Creek for the holiday festival?"

"My goodness child, you are packed to overflowing with things running through that little mind of yours." Nettie got up to wash the potatoes before cutting them in squares for boiling. She quickly sampled the pinto beans before sitting back down, pot in tow. "To answer your question child, Sleepy Creek is always running over with Christmas guest. It's been that way ever since the first festival, over two hundred years ago."

"Grandma, is it true nobody knows what happen to the Marshall family? Bobby Fisher, Libby Fisher's son, told me their daughter was about my age when she disappeared." Hattie watched her grandma run water over the potatoes and placed them on the stove burner. "I ask Bobby if his mother knew her name since she knew her age. I think she read it in one of her old books in her library."

3

"Hattie dear, Libby Fisher probably read about the Marshall family in the town records. Owning the only bookstore in Sleepy Creek, Libby Fisher talked the city council in letting her expand her book shop, one floor up, to house a library. Then she insisted the historical records be placed there in her care." Nettie pushed her glasses up in place. "She is a very nice lady, but quite the bookworm." Nettie sit down and giggled like a school girl. "Libby thinks she knows everything there is to know, but there have been stories passed down through the Russel family that many of the town's folk don't know!"

A wink from her sweet old face brought Hattie out of her chair, as she walked with excitement by her grandma's side, she scrambled for words.

"Stories passed down? Like, all the way back when great-great granddad was alive?" Hattie's eyes were wide with questions as she placed her hand on her grandma's shoulder "Did great-great grandad pass down the secret of the Marshall's disappearance?"

"I'm afraid not child, except the fact that the little girl was spotted in town that very morning of their disappearance. The story goes she had walked with a friend to visit her daddy in his office in town. The very building grumpy old William F. Marshall calls his home." Nettie got up to cut off her potatoes "Why the old gentleman chose to live there instead of fixing up the big house is beyond me."

"Maybe it's far too big for one person to live in grandma, or…maybe Mr. Marshall is just as afraid of that old house as the rest of the town people." Hattie smiled at her granddad when he came through the back door, covered with snow.

"Gideon Russel, just march back out there on that porch and take off that coat and those smelly boots!" Nettie frowned at her smiling husband "You are tracking up my kitchen! Stop smiling old man before I go out to your barn and release every animal inside!"

Giving her a peak on the cheek, Gideon winked at his granddaughter and walked back to the inside porch. Hattie made her way over to where her grandma was mashing the potatoes and reached up to sample some on the masher. Lovingly, her grandma brushed her hand away.

"Our Thanksgiving supper will be ready soon enough, young lady." Nettie reached over in a platter of her famous sugar cookies and handed one to her granddaughter. "There, eat a cookie, that should hold your stomach a while."

"Thanks grandma!" Hattie took a big bite and licked her lips "You sure know how to make cookies grandma. I bet you learned how by your mama, right?"

"Don't you ever run out of question Hattie Russel?" she laughed and poured heavy cream in the potatoes and stirred. "You were asking about the Marshall child's name, it was Pattie and she was age ten when she vanished."

Hattie's ears perked up "Her name was Pattie, Pattie Marshall? Wow grandma, that's already a piece of the puzzle that's been missing!" she twisted her head to one side as she eyed her grandma perplexed. "Why has our family kept all these secrets from the rest of Sleepy Creek? Shouldn't they at least know her name?"

"My dear granddaughter..." Gideon had overheard the conversation between his wife and Hattie and knew the girl had been asking questions again "I will tell you why the town people have not been informed about the things we know to be a fact! Your great granddad Aaron, went to the town squire one Christmas Eve to share that very story, a gift to Sleepy Creek, he called it. He said the town was swarming with visitors that particular festival, everyone was in the holiday spirit! The snow had been plentiful throughout the entire season, from Thanksgiving all the way to Christmas. As Aaron told the stories passed down through his father, the people grew restless, as if the mention of the name Marshall was a ghost from Christmas past, so they began singing Christmas carols loudly, to drown out my father. The story was never offered again. Father said he just stood there under the town's Christmas tree, it's colored lights shining in the dark, trying to calm down the sad feeling that gripped his soul."

"Do you suppose the people were afraid because it had grown dark and they really thought the ghost of Christmas past was standing just within that big old mansion, any moment to swoop down and make them vanish!" Hattie's heart was thumping in her chest, so many questions bottled inside to so many mysteries.

"Perhaps they were afraid of the darkness, like most of the town folk even today." Gideon scratched his chin, as if in thought "I suppose they could have been thinking about that dark gloomy house up on the hill. Sitting up there staring down on all the festivities. There are a lot of superstitious people in Sleepy Creek, Hattie, and that's a fact!"

5

"How 'bout you, granddad, are you superstitious? Do you think there's something living inside that old house? A ghost maybe?" Hattie followed him around the room as he went to wash up, as he called it. "If there is a ghost in that house, who could it be? One of the missing Marshalls or..." her eyes grew big "all the missing family?"

"As for starters young lady, I am not superstitious, not now, not ever! As for ghost living inside that dilapidated old ruin, I think the only thing living there are mice and spiders, having the freedom to come and go without so much as a..." he bent down in Hattie's face as he said quietly "Boo!"

"Granddad?" Hattie giggled and looped her arms around his neck. "Get serous! I, for one, think there's something living up on that hill, inside that shut off mansion. Whatever it is, must be hiding behind those old dark shutters and you know what else I think?"

"What possibly could our little Hattie be thinking, A big bad demon terrorizing our innocent little town?" Matthew walked in the kitchen and ran his fingers through his sister hair.

"Matthew Russel! I'll get you!" Hattie grabbed the flyswatter hanging on the back of the kitchen door and gave her brother a smack on the head. "Take that, smart alack! I'll find out what's hiding in that big house! You'll see!"

Hattie Marie Russel, you'll do no such thing!" Carolyn Russel had overheard her children's conversation when she walked in from the pantry, carrying the china for the table setting. "I do not have time to discuss this right now Hattie, but you will not be snooping around that strange old house! Just clear your mind of the very idea!" Hattie's mother carried the china to the large dining room table and called back "Besides, Mr. Marshall has strictly forbidden anyone to go near that place!"

"Your mama's right baby girl, that old house is dangerous. The floors are probably rotten and God knows what varmints might be calling it home." Hattie's daddy picked her up like she as a doll. His strong muscles shown clearly under his shirt.

"Hattie, your mama and daddy are both right, the old Marshall mansion is no place for a little girl." Nettie took her granddaughter hands and held them out, where she placed the bowl of mash potatoes. "Now, take this carefully to the table and go fetch the rest of your brothers, it time to eat." She bent down and kissed her, and in a whisper said

"We can talk more about the Marshall mystery another day Hattie, I promise! But now, it's time to thank our gracious Lord for another good harvest!"

Hattie smiled brightly at her grandma. "Thanks grandma. It's going to be a great Christmas in Sleepy Creek after all!" she carried the tempting bowl to the table then dashed off for her brothers.

Chapter 2

Thanksgiving had come and gone, the start of the Sleepy Creek's big Christmas celebration got into full swing. The town was overflowing with excited tourist as they joined in all the many activities planned and the overwhelming Christmas decorations. Every business was ablaze with Christmas lights, garland, and wreaths. The many homes that lined the neat streets were also decked out in their own radiant Christmas displays. The Russel family was no exception.

The big white farm house glowed with the window candles and the giant wreaths that rung proudly on their front door and on each of the barn's doors. The family, as had every generation of Russel's, picked out the perfect Christmas tree from their forest, to place in the big den, for the family to enjoy. As well as those who chose to come by for the Nettie Cookie Factory's open house, held on the second Saturday in the December.

Hattie Lay comfortably on her stomach in front of the warm fireplace, watching the logs burn away as they crackled and popped. She could hear everyone in her family chatting about the coming open house and the number of cards they had received so far from distant relatives. Hattie's young mind was on many things, like what gifts to buy this year for her parents, grandparents, and eight older brothers, who always made fun of her choice for them. With her meager allowance she received each year from gathering the chicken eggs and helping weed the vegetable garden in the summer time, Hattie had a hard time finding the perfect gifts.

The main thing that stayed perched in her head was the mystery of the Marshall family. For some reason, unbeknown to the ten-year-old, was the strong pull from some unseen force, that kept nagging for her to investigate and find out the truth. Hearing one of her brothers say "The Marshall mansion" Hattie sit up to hear what he was saying.

"Sure mama, I know you've warned us to stay away from that place, but the guys made a pack, to go see for ourselves!" Phillip glanced at his brothers, sensing their disapproval at his revelation in how the brothers slipped up to the old mansion on the night of Halloween to witness for themselves the strange light. "Mama, we're sorry we went against your order, but the Brower Boys kept calling us cowards and chickens!"

"So, you let these bullies get under your skin." Grandpa Russel tried to keep a stern face, while in truth he was proud of the boys standing up to the Brower's. "Did the Brower boys tell you they had seen the light from the attic?"

"They kept bragging about seeing the light, granddad." Andrew, the oldest spoke up in defense "The little jerks kept pushing us around and laughing in our face, especially…" his gaze fell on his mother "when we told him we were honoring our mama's request."

"Yeh, that's when they started calling us mama's boys!" James stood up next to his brother Philip "We love you mama, but we had to show those guys we were men and no chickens!"

"It was the perfect night to go, the moon was full, so we figured the light would really be shining bright." Simon spoke up nervously "It did!"

Hattie jumped up and grabbed Simon's arm with excitement "You saw the light? The mysterious light that comes from the attic?"

"It was the weirdness sight I have ever seen Hattie!" Simon's eyes grew wide as he remembered looking up from the scary front yard surrounding by giant oak trees, casting eyrie shadows on the old mansion. "I thanked God I had all my brothers there for support!"

"What did the light look like?" Hattie looked around the room at her eight brothers, feeling left out of the excitement "Are you going back?"

"Hattie, Simon is right, the light did appear weird looking, like no light I have ever seen." Andrew got up and walked up next to his little sister "I can tell you one thing, it didn't look like a reflection off broken glass, that's for sure."

"Refection off broken glass? Is that what those Brower brothers told you it was?" Hattie's head was swimming with unanswered questions.

"Hattie dear, your brother is referring to the deputy's report a few years back." Grandma Nettie had been knitting in her rocker as she listened to her grandson's great adventure and proud of them for standing up to the Brower's. "The town's people were in an uproar over the strange sighting coming from the old attic. They insisted the sheriff investigate the old mansion and find out what was causing the light to appear at night."

"It was that nosey bookworm, Libby Fisher, who headed up the committee to push Sheriff Sharp into doing his job, as she so gracefully put it." Granddad Gideon looked up from reading the newspaper "The delightful woman threatened him by announcing the elections would be coming up in November and he was up for re-election."

"Didn't Mr. Marshall order everyone to stay off his property?" Hattie looked at her grandpa in deep thought "How could Sheriff Sharp investigate if he couldn't get inside that old house?"

"Joe Sharp knew Mrs. Fisher meant business, so the reluctant sheriff paid the owner of Marshall Mills a visit, prepared with a search warrant." Gideon Russel gave a small chuckle, trying to imagine the nervous sheriff standing before the town's big grouch. "Reading over the legal paper, the angry owner of the old mansion agreed to one visit only."

"Our brave sheriff sent his two deputies out to the old Marshall house to investigate the mysterious light." Hattie's daddy remembered hearing about the funny situation. "Sharp insisted they go on a night when the moon was full to be sure the light would be visible, if it even existed, he had his doubts."

"If he didn't believe people's stories about the light, why was he too big a chicken to go there himself?" Hattie played with her ponytail nervously, wanting to hear more so she could find another piece to the puzzle.

"To be honest darling, our dear sheriff is afraid of his shadow." Nettie found it amusing "He only got elected in the first place because his father is the town mayor." Her old eyes crinkled with a big smile "Those two deputies were just as reluctant as their boss about visiting the old place in the dark, but they had their orders. So, Bud Rollins and Teddy Foster found themselves standing on the front lawn, shaking in their boots when the light appeared in the attic window."

"So, I reckon they went inside that old mansion in the dark with only flash lights!" Hattie's eyes grew wider as she tried to picture the two officers unlocking the big door and hearing the screeching sound when it opened. "That must have been real scary, especially going up those rickety dark steps to the attic!"

"I am sure it would have been frightening to step inside that old mansion after two hundred years, But, those two brave officers decided to wait until daylight before entering the mysterious house. They climb inside their patrol car, locked the doors and finally fell asleep." Gideon got up to put another log on the fire, then turned to warm his hands behind his back. "The next morning, the two officers made their way slowly up on the old porch where they found the floor in fairly good condition. With more confidence, they went inside, tossed a coin to see who would climb the stairs first, then Bud Rollins led the way to the attic. Looking around, they saw some broken glass lying just under the window and assumed that was where the strange light was reflecting off of. Case solved!"

"Not so fast grandpa, Andrew said that light couldn't be from some broken glass!" Hattie made her case "I think there's something else in that old attic causing that strange glow."

"That's it Hattie, it didn't shine like a regular light, it was more like a glow, right fellows?" Simon smiled down at his sister, feeling really proud she found the word to describe what they saw on Halloween night.

"That's exactly what it was! A glow that seem to grow bigger and brighter when midnight rolled around."

"Wow! I just gotta see that light! Andrew can we all go back on Christmas Eve, that's the next full moon. I read it in the paper!" Hattie felt her mama's hand on her shoulder.

"Hattie Marie, you may not go to the Marshall mansion on Christmas Eve or any night for that matter!" Taking her daughter by her shoulders, she turned her to face the staircase "Just march yourself upstairs and get ready for bed! We've got a busy day ahead of us tomorrow! Saturday after thanksgiving is one of our busiest days at the cookie factory and your father has to get the winter produce ready to take to the town square market! Scoot!"

"Yes mama, I'm going." Hattie made her way slowly up the steps to her room. Being the only girl gave her one good thing, her own private room and bath. She climbed into her long flannel gown, brushed her teeth and picked out her favorite book before getting under the sheets.

As she was settling in, Hattie heard her door open and her grandma Nettie peeked in smiling.

"I came to tuck you in child." She walked over and sat on the side of Hattie's bed, placing a cool hand on the girl's face. "Don't look so glum Hattie, I've got lots of stories about the Marshall family."

Hattie sat straight up, her face lit up in a brilliant smile.

"Do tell me grandma, everything you know!"

"In the morning child, after we see everyone has their breakfast and send them off to work." She bent over and kissed her granddaughter's cheek "Now, read until you're sleepy, then close those eyes! Morning will be here before you know it."

"Oh, I'm far too excited to read now, grandma!" Hattie pulled her covers up around her neck, reached over and switched off the lamp beside her bed. "I think I'll just lie here and put the Marshall puzzle together as I know it! When I get all the pieces grandma, I can solve the mystery!"

"I just think you might Hattie! Yes, indeed!" Nettie smiled as she closed the bedroom door, leaving Hattie Russel trying to scramble the few pieces of the mystery puzzle in her head, until at last she dropped off to sleep, dreaming about standing outside the old Marshall mansion to witness for herself the strange glow coming from the attic window.

Chapter 3

Hattie made her rounds pouring orange juice for her big family as they sat around the big harvest table that sit by the kitchen window. Her stomach was filled with butterflies as she anxiously waited for her family to finish their breakfast and head off to the jobs. She had been longing to hear more about the Marshall's and she was sure her grandma must have had tons of stories to tell. Her young eyes caught movement from the window and she squealed with delight.

"Look yall, it's snowing!" her southern slang sprang from her mouth "It's coming down in bushels!"

"It is, look everyone, it's snowing." Carolyn Russel corrected her daughter, having studied to be an English teacher before meeting and falling in love with Aaron, a farmer from the foothills of North Carolina. "I'm glad you boys got those new snow tires on our van yesterday. The weather man did say we might get four to five inches before this front, passes by."

"I'll hook the covered trailer to the tractor and drive that to the market this morning." Aaron reached for another biscuit and cut it in half for his butter, "These festival pilgrims never let a little snow stand in their way. I think it just brings out their Christmas spirit and everyone who has a stand in the square are rewarded from good sales, wouldn't you agree pop?"

"Spend, spend, spend...buy...buy...buy, like there's no tomorrow! Pass the gravy James!" after getting a big scoop, he smiled down at his granddaughter "Hattie, you and grandma gonna build a snowman after we get out of your hair?"

"We might grandpa if we finish our chores." Hattie tried to talk with her mouth full of biscuit "I always have fun with grandma, what with one thing or another, right grandma?"

"Right you are child" her old eyes twinkled as she started clearing away empty bowls "Now that your mama took my place at the factory, my happy job is to keep you busy and out of trouble when you're out of school."

Hattie watched as everyone got up from the table. She raced

over to collect the empty plates, thinking, as soon as we clean these things up, grandma can tell me stories about the Marshall family. She turned from the sink and watched her grandpa slip on his big winter coat. He gave Hattie a big smile as his wife wrapped his scarf securely around his neck and placed the big furry hat on top his white head.

"Boys, I'll wait for you in the barn. Your grandma has me wrapped up like I'm an Eskimo living at the North Pole!" he winked at Hattie "If I see Santa, I'll tell him what a good little girl you have been!" catching the look of Carolyn's disapproval, the old man chuckled and opened the covered porch door. He turned before leaving, a sly gleam in his eye "Alright boys, y'all hurry it along!" winking at Hattie, who was trying to restrain from giggling, he walked out whistling.

The house grew quiet as her family split up into two parties, her mama with Andrew, Peter, John, and Simon, her daddy and grandpa, with Philip, James, Matthew, and Thomas. Hattie felt like she would surely pop like a balloon if they didn't finish cleaning all the dirty dishes left from breakfast. She tried to get her mind off the mystery as she spoke up.

"I can't believe I've got to go back to school Monday, grandma. Crackling corn! I feel like we just got out for Thanksgiving!"

"Don't go fretting about school child. You'll be out before you can say shew fly!" Nettie looked around at the empty sink beside her "God be praise, all done!"

"That's great! Will you tell me some more of the mystery now grandma?" Hattie's eyes were round as saucers. "You promised!"

"That I did, Hattie, my girl." Making her way to the pantry for some dry peas, Nettie could hear her granddaughter close behind her. Pulling a big bowl down from a shelf, she placed it in Hattie's hands. "Hold this child while I scoop out some peas from the barrel."

"I'm dying to hear all about Pattie Marshall! Do you know more about her grandma?" Hattie followed behind her loving grandparent and placed the bowl in front of her after she took her seat, placing an empty pot on the table.

"Fresh goober peas for supper, simmered with a big chunk of fat back!" picking up her first dry pea, she began shelling as she licked her lips "Yum, there's nothing any better."

14

The Box in the Attic

"Grandma? Pattie Marshall?" Hattie started to sit next to Nettie when the older woman pointed to a large box sitting safely on the buffet. "Fetch that box of Christmas cards child and set them at the end of the table. Must not mess them up with these peas. Go up to my desk and get those Christmas stamps from the top drawer. You can pace them on while I tell you about Pattie Marshall and her best friend."

"Jumping jelly beans!" Hattie raced off for the stamps and came back to the table and slid excitedly onto her chair, pulling out the first of many, Christmas cards. "Is this the same friend who was reported walking in town with Pattie?"

"The same, and this should put a spark in those brown eyes, her friend's name was...Hattie Russel, your great-great aunt!" Nettie smiled when her granddaughter almost jumped out of her chair. "Are you speechless child?"

"Hat...Hattie Russel? She had...my name?" this came as a surprise to young Hattie as she sat staring at her grandma.

"Actually dear, you have your great-great aunt's name." her old eyes twinkled, knowing she had more surprises for the young sleuth "Your dear grandpa was always hoping for a girl to be born again in the Russel family so he could use her name. The first Hattie Russel was quite a pistol, much like you are. Always full of questions and Lordy me, talented, that girl could draw and write like the greatest, mind you."

"I wish I had known her grandma, she sounds real cool!" Hattie relaxed after she found out this woman she was named after was a pretty remarkable person. "So, Aunt Hattie was Pattie Marshall's best friend?"

"They were the best of friends, inseparable. It didn't matter to Pattie that her friend didn't come from a rich family, like herself." Nettie looked thoughtful "That dear sweet girl looked on the inside. She had a heart of pure gold and the day she disappeared was the saddest day in Hattie's life."

"What happen when Aunt Hattie walked with Pattie to town? Like, when did she see her last?" Hattie continued to put stamps on the large stack of cards.

"Let's go back a ways to the day Pattie and her mother came by the farmhouse to bring Hattie an early Christmas present." Nettie carried the pot of peas to the sink and filled it with water as she

15

thought. "It was the best gift the poor farm girl had ever received." "Tell me grandma, what did Pattie give her?" Hattie laid down the stamps and sit up, ears perked. "Her very own personal diary, with her name imbedded in gold on the cover." Placing the fat back deep within the peas, she put the lid on, then the burner. "Along with a quail pen and a large jar of black ink, to write down all her special memories from each day." "That was one swell present! You wouldn't know where she left her diary, would you grandma?" Hattie returned to her stamping "There could be some really neat clues in there to help me piece this mystery puzzle together!"

"Some people choose to be buried with their private diary, not wanting anyone to read their personal thoughts and memories." Nettie could see the blood draining from her granddaughter's face, as her disappointment was apparent. "But this was not the case with our Hattie!"

"She wasn't buried with her diary, lying far underground, never to be seen again?" Hattie jumped out of her chair and was by her grandma's side in a flash "If it's not in the grave with her, where is it? Please, tell me you know grandma."

"Hattie Russel's diary is tucked safely away, in an old chest, along with some of her things…" Nettie's eyes grew wide with excitement "Up in the attic!"

Chapter 4

"Tumbling turnip greens! Not the old attic in the haunted mansion! The place with the mysterious glowing light!" Hattie felt her skin crawl at the thought.

"Heaven's sake child, what would your Aunt's things be doing in that locked up place?" Nettie took her granddaughter's hand "Come with me up to the attic. I'll show you where they were placed after her death." As they made their way up to the attic, Nettie continued to speak "It was Hattie's request that her precious diary be put away in the old chest after her death, along with her prize possessions. Then she ordered it locked until such time another Hattie Russel was born, to solve the mystery of their mysterious disappearance on Christmas Eve, 1814."

"Wow! It was two hundred years ago!" Hattie's eyes grew big when her grandmother opened the attic door and switched on the single light, that dangled down on a wire from the highest rafter. She looked around, casing the room for what looked like a chest. Hattie had been in the attic many times, getting Christmas decorations out and putting them back up until the next year. Her curiosity of what she might find, caused her to wonder around as the other family members carried things down stairs to the big den. Thinking back to past exploring, she could not recall seeing a chest up in the attic.

Hattie's grandmother made her way to a far corner, where she removed a board from the floor and pulled up the chest.

"Here it is, Hattie Russel Martin's chest, not opened until this day!" Nettie was growing as anxious as her young granddaughter when she waved the frozen girl over. "Well Hattie, are you ready to see what inside the chest?"

"I'm more than ready grandma!" she made her way through the stakes of boxes and old furniture, too torn up to repair, until she stood trembling, gazing down at the chest. "No wonder I never saw it before, it was well hidden. It's locked grandma! Do you know where they hid the key?"

"Does peanut butter like jelly?" her old eyes came alive as she placed an old stool under the middle rafter "Climb up here Hattie and feel carefully with your hand on top of the main rafter. They say that is where the key was placed."

Climbing carefully on the old stool, held firmly by her grandma, Hattie reached up and slowly moved her fingers until they touched something cold. It felt like metal. Lifting it carefully as not to drop it in a crack on the old floor, Hattie slowly brought the object down. She took a deep breath then opened her fingers and smiled down at the gold key.

After carrying the chest down to the kitchen table, Nettie told her delighted granddaughter to unlock the old chest. With shaky fingers, Hattie slipped the gold key inside the lock and with a snap, it popped open.

"Now to see what's inside!" Hattie's smile was as big as her grandmother's when she slowly opened the lid "Holy ravioli! Look grandma, there's all sorts of drawings in here and..." she lifted the stack of art from its resting place and laid them gently on the table for further viewing, her young eyes falling on a pretty red dress, trimmed in green holly and berry lace. "It's a Christmas dress!" Hattie handed it to her grandma who gently unfolded it and held it up.

"This dress didn't come from your aunts last fashions, Hattie. I'd say, she wore this dress when she was around your age." Nettie turned the long dress around and admired the big white bow at the waist. "I would guess, this being the only garment in the chest, this dress held some sentimental value to the young girl. What would be your guess Hattie?"

"Putting myself in Aunt Hattie's shoes, I think this was the last dress she wore when she was with her dearest friend, Pattie." Hattie looked at the pretty dress, tilting her head from side to side "She cherished her last memory with her best friend and it's obvious Hattie thought about her often, wondering what happen to her. That is why, her dying wish was to place all her most precious possessions in the chest until a new Hattie could solve the mystery of her best friend's disappearance! Me!"

"You have become quite the detective Hattie Russel!" Nettie chuckled and grew silent when she watched her granddaughter slowly lift out the beautiful diary with Hattie Russel richly written in pure gold. At the bottom of the chest was a few pieces of jewelry and the old pen and ink well, long used or dried up from the attic heat. "You found it!"

"Jumping Jupiter! How many clues do you have written down, Great-Great Aunt Hattie?" Hattie turned to her grandma who was watching her closely. "Would you like me to read it out loud grandma? I know you must be anxious to hear what Hattie wrote!"

"I wouldn't dream of missing one single word child." The older woman stood up on shaky legs, not use to climbing the attic stairs. "But first, I need to fix us a quick lunch. It's past twelve already and I need to check on my peas."

"Golly gee, grandma, I'm nearly busting inside, for the need to read this diary! How could you possibly eat right now grandma? I'm just full and simply running over with excitement! Can't we skip lunch and fill up on words?"

"My goodness child, must you always let everything sound like it's do or die!" Nettie Russel lifted a jar of peanut butter from the cupboard, along with a jar of grape jelly. "I'm making your favorite, peanut-butter and jelly sandwich and a cold glass of milk!"

"Grandma, how do you expect me to read this diary with my mouth glued with peanut butter?" Hattie propped up on her elbows, obviously disappointed. She watched her grandmother set the sandwiches down and go back for the milk. "Grandma?"

"Hattie, what I expect is for you to push that book out of harm's way and eat your lunch! Now bow you head for grace." Smiling as Hattie gave in and lowered her head, Nettie prayed "Dear Lord, help my head strong granddaughter to have patience and to respect her elders. Thank you for these lovely sandwiches and milk..." she peeked up to see the child squirming in her seat "and please Lord, let Hattie find lots of clues in the Marshall mystery and help her solve their strange disappearance. Amen!"

"Amen and amen!" Hattie sat up and dived into her sandwich, feeling better about upsetting her sweet grandmother. "Thank you, grandma, for asking the Lord to help me! I can always use His help, after all, if anyone knows what happened, it's God and his Holy angels, right?"

"There is nothing our creator does not know child, but don't be getting up your hopes that he will tell you out right what happen! Just because you can't hear him tell you, does not mean he's not going to help you."

19

"But how grandma, how can He help me solve this case all by myself?" Hattie washed down her sandwich as she waited for her grandmother to respond.

"From the Holy Spirit, Hattie. He will put thoughts in your head to guide you to clues, like giving your aunt the wisdom to write down everything she witnessed." Nettie got up to clear the table, glad Hattie's thoughts were not completely on reading the diary. "If William Franklin Marshall was a wee bit friendly. I'm sure he could tell you things he must know. After all, he is the last living relative. When he dies, so goes everything he knew. It might even solve this case."

"Are you saying, grumpy old Marshall of Marshall Mills might know what happen to Pattie and her family?" Hattie's eyes grew wide with suspicion.

"Not just the Marshalls my dear, their entire staff disappeared at the same time, and they had quite a staff, a cook, a butler, two house maids, a personal maid for each of the Marshalls, a chauffeur, and a gardener."

"Rolling snow balls! That means there's nine people missing!" Hattie reached for the diary "It's time to find out what's written inside this diary grandma, to see how many pieces can be added to the puzzle." She slowly turned to the first page, dated, December 22, 1814.

"Dear Diary!...

Chapter 5

"December 22, 1814 Dear Diary, today was a very exciting day! My very best friend, Pattie Marshall paid us a visit, along with her mother! They came in a fancy carriage, driven by what they called, their chauffeur. I think that's just a fancy name for coachman. Pattie surprised me with an early Christmas gift, wrapped in exquisite red paper adorned by a huge white bow! It was about the prettiest gift I have ever seen! The only gift, I thought, that could have been better, was the gift of our Savior on that first Christmas!

My fingers were so nervous when I unwrapped it, I was much afraid that I might drop it. To my delight, I managed to get the paper off in one piece, so that I might save it. Oh, Dear Diary, when I saw you with my name in solid gold, mind you, on your cover, I thought I might die, right there, from pure happiness!

I couldn't thank my friend enough, as I must have worn her out repeating thank you and smothering her in grateful hugs!

Pattie is the most thoughtful person I know. She told me, she wanted me to have my very own diary early so I could write down all our special times together, starting with the holiday season. I felt really bad that I hadn't even gotten my present to her yet. Daddy wouldn't get paid at the mill until Friday and had promised me one whole dollar to get Pattie a special gift. I hope I can find her that special gift only friends can share. I know Pattie will love anything I give her, no matter the cost because she loves me and I love her!

I didn't think my heart could hold anymore joy until I heard Mrs. Marshall ask my mother if I could come back with them to have a sleep in with Pattie! When I heard mama say I could, I thought I would pop, right in two.

Mama took me up to my room to help me pack my overnight cloth bag and surprised me with yet another early Christmas gift, a new flannel sleeping gown, to take with me instead of my old one, which was too short cause I had been growing.

So, happily, I'm writing this tonight at a small desk in Pattie's bedroom by a flickering candle. I must say, diary, her room is four times bigger than mine and she has a very large canape bed, covered with the finest bed coverings anyone living in Sleepy Creek have ever seen!

We had a most delightful supper this evening, they call it 'dinner', I guess people that's rich call it that, it's all the same thing. Some of the dishes looked too good to eat, but I enjoyed them anyway.

Pattie's parents are very sweet and kind to me. I suppose it's because Pattie loves me so much. Her daddy seemed a little sad and didn't have much to say, but when he hugged Pattie at bedtime and told her he loved her, I thought that was terribly sweet.

Pattie told me something before she fell asleep, she said it was a secret and never mention it to anyone. Pattie is afraid for her father and said he was depressed because he was turning forty. She thinks he fears dying at a young age, like his father and his grandfather who died in their early fifties. He has trouble sleeping and has a nagging fear of night time. Pattie even admitted she had grown afraid of her father, especially at night so she started having her personal maid sleep in her room with her.

Maybe things will look brighter in the morning, but for now my eyes are growing heavy so I must close my first entry. Hattie Russel."

"Creeping crawling corn snakes! There seem to be plenty of clues already, and that's just the first entry grandma!" Hattie heard the tall grandfather clock in the entrance hall strike three and she knew the men folk would be coming through the back door pretty soon. "Oh, rats! We only read one day from the diary and it's time for grandpa and daddy!"

"Then this will be the perfect time for you to scoot up to your room and write down the theories you have come up in the first writing. Once we finish reading all of the ones pertaining to this case, you can start putting the pieces together." Nettie got a big smile from her granddaughter, knowing she approved the suggestion.

"Alright Hattie, what clues have you gotten from the first entry in Aunt Hattie's diary?" All the Russel family had retired to the rooms for the night, exhausted from their busy day. Hattie had begged her grandmother to come by her room, so they could read the next entry in Hattie's diary. Sitting up in bed, Nettie nestled beside her in a comfy chair, Hattie opened her note book containing her notes about the case.

"The first clue is receiving the early Christmas gift from her friend. Pattie wanted Hattie to have her diary before the holidays, to start recording what was happening." Hattie spoke with excitement in her voice, keeping it low, as not to wake her family. "It's as if Pattie knew something was about to happen, but she wasn't sure what.

The second clue was Mrs. Marshall asking Aunt Hattie to come home with them for a sleep over with her friend. This was a busy time of the year for everyone in Sleepy Creek, especially the owners of the Mill, Christmas holidays being one of their busiest times for shipping out all the woolen garments they made, including, I'm sure, Aunt Hattie's new flannel gown." Hattie ran her hand down her long gown "Much like this one from Marshall Mills."

"They do stay busy in the winter time, starting in the early fall." Nettie remembered the old mill when she was a child and it hadn't changed in her lifetime. Nettie knew it was the very same building the first William Marshall had built in Sleepy Creek. As a matter of fact, most of the buildings and houses in the small town, were just as old. "Maybe Pattie's parents felt their daughter could use something to take her mind off of her parent's long hours with the mill work. The story goes, Susanne Marshall, Pattie's mother did most of the book keeping at home for Marshall Mills in her private home office."

"Maybe, but I think Susanne Marshall knew her little girl was afraid of her daddy because she too could see the change in him and thought her best friend might distract her and take her mind off him." Hattie looked down at the third clue.

"And that brings me to the third clue. Pattie told Hattie about the change in her father, being afraid of dying in his fifties and the fear of night coming! Grandma, Pattie admitted she was so afraid of him, she had her personal maid move in with her. I think Pattie feared for her life!"

"Let's hope that wasn't the case child. God forbid that good family man hurt his only daughter, along with his wife and entire staff!" Nettie felt a cold chill race down her spine at the very thought.

"This sudden fear that gripped Mr. Marshall could have driven him mad, insane. Crazy enough to plan a way to take his own life, along with everyone in his household." Hattie looked thoughtful

"Aunt Hattie said he looked sad and was very quiet when she was around him."

"Well, maybe the next entry will clear up some of these questions." Nettie pulled her chair closer to the bed. "Are you ready to read more?"

"More than ready grandma!" Hattie turned to the second page and began reading.

December 23, 1814, Dear Diary, I'm writing this tonight in my bedroom, by my bedside stand and with a used worn, down candle, so I best write fast, unless I intend to write it by the almost full moon.

The morning looked a lot brighter in Pattie's big bedroom and she seem to be in better spirits. We sat in bed for a while, chatting about Mark Russel, one of my brothers. Four years Pattie's senior. She really has a big crush on him but made me promise not to mention a word of it to him or anyone. To make her feel good, I told her I thought Mark had sparks for her as well. I have never seen a bigger brighter smile befall my dear friend's lips from one small revelation. I never told her a fib, Dear Diary, my brother is smitten with my friend, he just won't admit it.

Breakfast was served in what they called the 'breakfast room', a bright room, surrounded by large windows and lots of potted plants, almost as big as a small tree! It was a scrumptious meal, with ham, eggs, some kind of fancy potatoes, melons and real fresh squeeze orange juice. Instead of biscuits or a hoecake like mama bakes, they had something called, French crescents, they were very good!

Pattie's daddy didn't join us for breakfast. Mrs. Marshall said he was called down to his town office, some sort of meeting. Pattie and I were having a wonderful time, playing with all her beautiful dolls when her maid came up and told her to put on her outer wear. Mr. Torrance, their driver, had orders to take her to town to pay her father a visit. I could tell Pattie was nervous about going and she ask if I would accompany her.

When we got to town, there were a lot of people in the streets, celebrating the holiday festival, so the big carriage could not get past the first block. I suggested we walk the rest of the way to her father's office and she agreed. I think Pattie was glad for our time alone so she could talk about her worry's why her father really wanted her to come down without her mother, who had always joined her in visits to his office.

Mr. Marshall seem to be in a merrier spirit when we arrived in his office. He was laughing and singing the Christmas Carol, Hark, the Herald Angels Sing! He had his secretary fix some hot Apple cider drink for us. Then after I drank my last drop, he told me that he would be seeing his daughter home and he would have Mr. Torrance to drive me back to the big house for my things and take me home. Taking my hand, he walked me to the door where Mr. Torrance stood waiting. I looked back to see if Pattie was alright. She was sitting on her father's knee, deep into a conversation I could not hear. Pattie looked my way, waved and blew me a kiss and I came home, feeling somewhat sad. I cannot put my finger why I feel so strange, as if I might never see my dearest friend again. Perhaps it's just the coming of the full moon on Christmas Eve that has me in the unusual mood. It will be better in the morning, it's always brighter then.   Hattie Russel."

"Did you discover any clues in that reading Hattie?" Nettie could tell her granddaughter was lost in thoughts. "Hattie, did you hear what I said or are you just getting weary." The older woman checked her watch "Lordy me, it's half pass eleven, I'm getting tired myself. Best turn in."

Hattie sit, staring at the last words, much to excited to be sleepy as she finally looked over at her grandmother.

"Grandma, Hattie had the feeling something bad was going to happen to her friend and it had something to do with the full moon, on Christmas Eve." Hattie gently closed the diary, her young mind still thinking "The answers lie inside that old house grandma! What ever happen to the Marshalls and their entire staff happened on Christmas Eve, all at the same time! There's something glowing from that attic and whatever it is, will help me solve this mystery, I just know it!"

"Hattie, you know your mama forbids you to go anywhere near that old house!" Nettie reached over and touched her hand "It's not safe child."

"If I'm ever going to get to the bottom of their disappearance grandma, That's my last hope, but how?" Hattie pushed the covers back and slung her feet around to face her dear grandma "If I could only convince mean old William Marshall to let me go in, I could search that old attic and find out the secret."

"I suppose if you got the old grouch's permission, your mama might not object so much, only, of course, if you take your brothers." Nettie knew Hattie was far too excited to go to sleep.

"Grandma, this is my case! Besides those brothers of mine will just make fun of me! I promise not to go alone. Who knows, maybe Mr. Marshall himself will accompany me."

"At least wait until after the Christmas Season child, it's far too busy around here and even for Mr. Marshall now." She stood up and helped her granddaughter back under her covers "Now get some sleep." She blew her a kiss and cut out the light before slipping out the door.

Hattie lay there in the dark, staring out the window at the almost full moon.

"The moon will be full on Christmas Eve, same as it was when the Marshall's disappeared. It's got to be Christmas Eve when I go to that old mansion! Somehow, someway, I will get into that house and go to the attic. I'll have the moonlight to guide me to the thing that glows up there!"

Chapter 6

Hattie woke up on Sunday morning and noticed the snow, falling softly outside her window. Her thoughts drifted back to December, 1814 and wondered if they had just as much snow that Christmas season. Looking at her bedside clock, Hattie knew her family would be getting out of bed and heading down for breakfast and the men folk, their morning milking, that never stopped to take a Sunday off. The cows needed milking and that was a fact!

Remembering sliding the precious chest under her bed the previous day, Hattie quickly got up and on her knees, were she retrieved the pretty gold box, filled with her aunt's treasures. She lifted it carefully on her bed and lifted the lid to peer inside. The stack of drawings had been returned to their resting place inside the chest, but the red Christmas dress hung safely inside Hattie's closet, so that the wrinkles would hopefully fall out, after so many years of being stored away.

Hattie carefully lifted up the first three drawings and recognized instantly the old Russel farm house as the first one. The second drawing was one of the old barn with a couple of milk cows and one big work horse. Picking up the third drawing, Hattie smiled down at a black and white cat with four small kittens, playing over the mother cat. The rest of the drawings, seven in all, were mainly of farm scenes or animals.

Her attention was moved to the diary, lying on her night stand and she walked over and picked it up.

"Diary, I would love to dive right into the next entry, but as tempting as the thought, I know I must wait until we get back from Church services and have our Sunday lunch right after!" Making her bed, Hattie slid the diary under her pillow, for safe keeping. "There! My brothers know my room is off limits to them, unless I invite them to come in!"

Hearing her mother call up the stairs announcing breakfast, Hattie quickly adorned her robe and went down to join the family.

"There's my girl! Ready for your breakfast? My Nettie's gravy is extra good this morning!" his callous hand rubbed over her head.

"You already finished your breakfast, grandpa?" Hattie watched him put on his old work coat and hat "Don't forget your woolen scarf, it's snowing again!"

"Looking after your old grandpa, are you?" Gideon Russel chuckled as he pulled down his warm scarf and wrapped it securely around his thin neck. "Snug as a bug in a rug! To answer your question sweet girl, I have indeed had my good hardy breakfast, so if you boys will move those forks a little faster, you may join me at the barn!"

"We're coming, grandpa!" Andrew drank down his milk and stood up, slapping his brother's gently on their head. "Milking time fellows! We got church this morning!"

"Time sure is flying us by! It feels like I was just putting on my suit and tie!' James, 17, didn't fancy dressing up and would have preferred wearing his school jeans to church. To please their mother, all eight boys decked out in their dark suits.

"I bet Emily Walters thinks you look real handsome on Sunday morning, little brother!" Peter, 19, walked to the door with Andrew, as one by one they hurried to catch up, James arguing all the way out.

"I wonder how many people will be at church this morning, mama? What with all that snow coming down and all!" Hattie carried the empty plates to the sink to wash, another chore, for girls.

"Hattie's got a point Mother Nettie." Carolyn tied the flowered apron over her winter day dress, her eyes going to the window were the early morning light had made it easier to see the big flakes coming down. "I guess those two dear widows, Mellie Robinson and Abigail Dunn, won't be coming this morning since their neighbor Drake Ashton fell at the mill and broke both his legs, poor soul."

"He is indeed a kind soul to offer those dear ladies a ride to church, especially when the weather is bad. Now he can't even take his wife and three little ones to church or anywhere else, for that matter." Nettie rinsed the dishes as Hattie washed, leaving Carolyn to dry and set aside. "I know that William F. Marshall is a hard man to work for, but to fire a loyal employee for missing work and because of a job he was ordered to do right there at the mill! Why, the big Scrooge should be sued for the dear man falling off that rotten latter!"

"And it would serve him rightly, Mother Nettie, if the crooked business man hadn't made each of his employees sign a waver, relieving himself of any responsibly pertaining to accidents at the job site."

"The grouchy old recluse has no heart to fire a man with a wife and three little children, right here at Christmas!" Nettie removed her old worn apron and hung it on a nail behind the door. "I guess Pastor Reavis will give us an update on their welfare."

"I'm sure he will have a list for anyone who can donate what the Ashton's need to help get them through until he gets back on his feet and finds new employment nearby." Carolyn took her daughter's hand who had been taking in all their exchanged words about Mr. Marshall, the man she had hoped might give his approval to investigate his old mansion. "You're mighty quiet Hattie, no questions from the girl who wants to know everything."

"I've learned mama, sometimes a detective can learn a lot, just by listening and taking notes, in their head." Hattie smiled over at her grandma when she heard her give a soft chuckle. "Well, I'm off to my room to get ready for church." She turned half way up the heart pine wooden steps, her eyes serious "Maybe there will be something on Pastor Reavis' list that I can share with the Ashton family! I'd like to help, do my part!" with that, Hattie raced inside her room to get dressed.

The church service was going into the Christmas story, starting with Mary finding out she was to be the mother of Jesus, our Savior. Hattie especially liked singing Christmas carols at long last and looking around at all the beautiful decorations which created a majestic glow near the altar. There the Holy Family sat, surrounded by candles and poinsettias, while candles burned warmly from each window-sill and the giant Christmas tree shone brightly with what appeared to be a million lights to the ten-year-old.

The last carol had been sung and Pastor Reavis walked down from the chancel with a sheet of paper in his hand.

"Christian brothers and sisters, I'm sure most of you have heard the news about brother Drake losing his job at the mill. It has put a strain on their savings and in short, my friends, his funds are almost exhausted. Mr. Ashton is too proud to ask for help but with the holidays approaching I'm certain this dear family could use our help." The preacher held up the list. "This is a list of things they must have to survive the cold winter and the staples they need to get by, such as food and medicines. Any fire wood you can spare will be a big blessing. Bedcoverings and warm clothing are a must. For those who have nothing material to share, we have also set up a fund for heating oil and to help with their electric bill."

He looked out over the congregation "I'm sure if one of us were in the same shoes as brother Ashton and his wife Hilda, we would welcome any help given lovingly by our Christian family. The list will be in the vestibule."

Hattie was proud to see what a great response was shone by the Sleepy Creek Methodist Church members and she felt all joyful inside for being a part of such a loving bunch of people, none of which had much money themselves.

The Russel's didn't talk much about the offerings they had written down at church for the Ashton family, but Hattie knew it had to be quite a lot from watching her parents and grandparents discussing it among themselves and from the amount of writing her mama was doing. So, at the lunch table, Hattie decided to find out.

"I feel really bad for the Ashton's, daddy. It looked like everyone at church was willing to help." Hattie measured her words carefully "Was there anything on that list I could do to help? They didn't let the kids see the list."

"Hattie dear, we gave plenty for the family." Carolyn looked up from her chicken "I'm sure the Russel's have done their fair share to help that poor family."

"Then what did we offer to give them mama?" Hattie kept her eyes on her food "I've got an old blanket I don't use anymore, perhaps…"

"Child, that is very sweet of you to offer your old blanket and I'm sure it would be appreciated, along with the two new ones from me and your mama." Nettie reached over and patted her granddaughter's head "It was our Christmas gift to one another this year, but we can wait until next Christmas for a new blanket. Besides, my old blanket has a lot of life left in it."

"Wow! Grandma, mama, that's most generous!" Hattie had several presents under the tree, not to mention what she would be asking Santa to bring, so the happy thought sprang out from her lips "I'm sure I must have a gift under the tree that I can give!"

"Such an unselfish young lady." Adam Russel looked

admiringly at his little girl "Those gifts are especially for you Hattie, but you are just as much a part of these gifts we're giving than anyone here around this table."

"Yes, she is, as are the boys, so I say they need to know what they're giving!" Gideon winked at his granddaughter. "For starters, a whole country ham from our smoke house, a couple dozen eggs per- week, enough milk to cook with and for the growing children. Several jars of Nettie's green beans, corn, tomatoes, beets, and strawberry preserves. Apples, peanuts, white potatoes, and sweet potatoes from the root cellar. Stacks of fire wood and kindle to warm their small house."

"I'd say that's about the most that family will receive from anyone at church!" Andrew stood up, feeling proud he had such a giving family. "I'll check and see if anyone put down a Christmas tree for them."

That's a swell idea Andrew!" Hattie sit up "We can ask if there's anyone who might have some lights and ornaments they could share.!

"I'll bring it up tonight at the M.Y.F. and see if the youth group want to make it our Christmas project this year!" John jumped up excited over the ideal "Last meeting we were lost for any new ideals. This will be perfect!"

"Yeh, we could even make some really neat ornaments ourselves! Some of the girls are good at crafts!"

"That sounds wonderful boys!" Adam got up to get the Sunday paper, glad everyone had gotten into the giving spirit. "If you need anything from the woods or barn, help yourself..." he smiled at his oldest child "Go ahead and pick out the perfect Christmas tree Andrew. You and Peter can carry it over and put it up for them after the youth come up with the lights and decorations"

Hattie felt left out as she slipped out and ran up to her bedroom to think.

"There must be something I can do to help, but what?" her eyes fell on her letter to Santa Clause "I've got it! I'll earn money to buy gifts for the three Ashton children. If I make enough, I can get their parents a Christmas gift as well to put under the tree!"

Hattie flopped down on her bed, trying to think of how she could possibly raise enough money for gifts when her time was running out. Absent mindedly, she gazed at the postcards her mother had printed advertising this year's prices for her famous cookies, to be handed out to people at the open house. Suddenly Hattie sit straight up, the brilliant ideal brightening up her face.

"I will sale cookies! Not just any cookie, but my very own secret cookie! Daddy can take me to the market and set me up a little stand. I'll inform everyone the sales will be going to help buy Christmas gifts for the Ashton family!" Too excited to sit, Hattie started pacing the floor, trying to come up with a catchy name for her cookie. Then it hit her, the perfect name. Her cookies would be called: Hattie's Patties!

Chapter 7

The day went by quickly as Hattie excused herself to go up a little early to read before turning in for the night. Tomorrow would bring her return to Sleepy Creek School for two more weeks, then she would have two weeks out for the Christmas holidays. It would be a busy time for the Russel family and the Nettie Cookie open house will take up a good part of the afternoon on Saturday, but Hattie had other ideals.

She smiled at her grandmother as she walked inside the bedroom, ready for another reading from the diary of Hattie Russel. With excitement, Hattie opened the old book and turned to the third page.

December 24, 1814 Dear Diary, Christmas Eve finally arrived today along with yet another beautiful snow. It seems to be falling practically every day this season, much to the delight of all the visitors in Sleepy Creek. The constant hustle and bustle has been going on ever since Thanksgiving and everyone seems to be having a joyful jolly time. All but me, my insides are having a sinking feeling over the disappearance of my dearest and best friend.

Pattie came by very early this morning bringing me yet another Christmas gift. I told her I felt really bad that her gift was not yet ready. I had been working on it ever since mama took me shopping to buy everything I needed. I knew Pattie's parents could buy her anything she wanted, so I wanted to give her something only I could give her.

Pattie often admired the paintings I had done of the farm and she told me I had a gifted talent from God. I'd never painted a person before, but when I put the brush to the canvas it came alive with our faces. This could be a gift to remind her heart, no matter how old she became, I would always be her very best friend. Now I had to simply wait for the paint to dry, then I would wrap it up in that pretty red paper she had mine in, along with the big white bow.

I promised my friend that I would bring it to church on Sunday or by her house if I got it ready sooner. my understanding friend never showed disappointment but I'm sure she must have been wondering what it could be. She simply said, "It will be special no matter what it is, it will be from you" then she asked me to wait and open my gift on Christmas morning. It felt very heavy and I couldn't imagine what it was, but I promised Pattie I would wait to open it.

The thing I can't understand diary, Pattie came alone, with only the coachman to bring her. She seemed to be nervous, as her attention was drawn down the road as though she was afraid of being followed. I ask her in for milk and cookies but to my disappointment, she said she had to get right back home. Dear Diary, my friend and I have always hugged goodbye before leaving one another, but this time was much different. Pattie hugged me real tight and it seem like an extra, long time to me, like she didn't want to let me go. I had a strange feeling she was in trouble and afraid to return home. Then as she was climbing back on the carriage, some unseen force had me to run after her and stop her. Setting her feet back down, she turned and smiled at me, then drew confused when I reached around my neck and removed my favorite neckless, a small wooden cross and placed it over her head.

Tears filled her beautiful blue eyes as her love for me spoke volumes, for she knew why the cross was so special to me, it was the last gift from my grandma Louise, my very favorite grandma, whose death broke my heart at age five. Pattie tried to remove it and give it back, knowing I had never taken it off, but I refused as the strangest words flowed out of my mouth. I said, "Dear friend, I know this is not gold or silver, nor was it of great cost, but the love it holds, outweighs any precious metals known to man. This cross is made from the dogwood tree, same as the cross on Calvary. Wear it to announce, you are a child of God! Wear it to announce, you are a follower of Jesus, our Savior. Wear it to announce, your heart is filled with the Holy Spirit and IT WILL KEEP YOU SAFE, always."

Dearest Diary, you know what I think? I think the Holy Spirit came into my heart and had me say those things to help Pattie's fear and I think, somehow, someway, my wooden cross will help save her. Pattie seemed to be in better spirits after those words and with one last hug, she left and I never seen her again.

I did get her painting finished and talked my daddy into dropping by the Marshall Mansion before we went to Christmas Eve services. Daddy let me run up to the big door while he and mama, along with my four brothers, waited in the wagon. I could hear piano music coming from their music room, so I knew they were home, yet as soon I began striking the knocker, the house fell silent and no one came to the door. Then I noticed the huge black shutters had been shut and locked on the inside. If there had been candles burning within the big house, I couldn't see them through the closed shutters.

I heard daddy call my name and I knew we would be late if I didn't go back to the wagon. As I turned to leave, a light, no a glow flickered in the attic. It gave me the chills watching it grow brighter as I stared up. I nearly jumped out of my skin when daddy touched my shoulder. I told him about hearing the music before knocking, then everything grew silent. Daddy said it was obvious no one was at home and I must have heard the wind through the young oak trees. When I told Daddy about the light, he looked up at the attic window and found it dark. Taking my hand, he pulled me to the wagon and said I would see Pattie at church.

Just as the wagon was driving away, I glanced back for one last look. The glow was back as well as something indescribable, staring from the window, looking straight at me! I closed my eyes to block out it's red eyes and when I opened them, the attic was dark. I only hope Pattie is alright and I can sleep this night.   Hattie Russel.

Hettie's hands trembled when she closed the diary and looked up at her bewildered grandmother.

"Gosh! Jumping horn frogs! I was right, there's something in that old attic grandma, something…alive!"

"Your Aunt Pattie could have imagined seeing some sort of demon in that window Hattie. Her little head was already spinning with worry for her friend's safety and sometimes shadows from trees cast an eyrie glow in dark windows." Nettie tried to calm down her granddaughter, hoping this reading wouldn't keep her awake. "Once, when I was around your age, I was outside in the growing darkness, playing 'Ain't no bears out tonight' when my eyes were drawn to our kitchen window. I could swear I saw a long black cat lying on the windowsill. It turned out to be granny Russel's long flower bed."

"I'm sorry grandma, but I believe Aunt Hattie really saw something evil staring at her from that attic window. A tree's shadow will not create two red eyes, nor would a grove of young oak trees be high enough to cast their shadow all the way up to the attic." Hattie opened the book back up and scanned down the words. "One of my questions were answered, in 1814 it snowed just as much as it has this season. Then there's the second Christmas gift from Pattie. It seemed to surprise Aunt Hattie that Pattie was giving her two gifts. I think up until then, they only exchanged one gift a piece."

"And you are probably correct child." Nettie marveled at her granddaughter's detective skills "The people in that day, unless they were very wealthy like the Marshalls. Couldn't afford to give lots of gifts like we tend to in our generation."

"What do you suppose was in the present? Hattie said it was heavy so it couldn't be one of her dolls." Hettie was tempted to turn the page and read Christmas day but she knew it was getting late and her grandma would never allow her to continue.

"The suspense will have to wait until you get home from school tomorrow young lady." Nettie gently retrieved the book and put it in her gown pocket and despite Hattie's groaning, she turned toward the door, smiling to herself. "Hattie Marie Russel, now don't you go fretting over me taking this book. I promise I will not so much as peek inside it. You need your rest! You've got school in the morning and I will not let you have this diary at your disposal. I know you pretty good, young lady. As soon As I leave for my room, you would have read that next chapter, right?"

Hattie gave her grandma a sheepish grin "It was tempting grandma."

"Then we see eye to eye!" the old woman's smile was bright "We'll read it right after you finish your homework. Deal?"

"Yes ma'am, it's a deal." Hattie mumbled, somewhat annoyed that her grandmother took her prize possession from her. She pulled her covers up and rolled over as the light was switched off by Nettie.

Hattie lay staring at the wall, thinking about going inside that old mansion alone. She shivered from a strange chill, despite her warm blankets. Coming to the conclusion she must not go there alone, she listed in her mind who she could trust with all her secrets.

"Of course, my best friends! Jane, Amy, and Bobby will be thrilled to be a part of my detective club." Hattie bit her lip with excitement "We will call our secret club, The Missing Piece! Brilliant, Hattie Russel!" she smiled and closed her eyes, the dark attic window came into focus "What's up in that attic? Who's up in that old attic, still breathing, still alive, still watching out for trespassers!"

Chapter 8

Hattie and her friends had met in the cafeteria to have lunch together and she thought this would be the perfect time to spring her ideal on them. She opened her milk and took a sip as she pulled out her ham biscuit from her brown sack.

"How would you guys like to join my secret detective club?" at once, all three popped up and looked over at their smiling friend. "Good!" she thought "I've got their undivided attention." Hattie wiped her lips "I've got a really great case and have several clues already!"

"Gosh Hattie, is it anything like the lost dog case, when we tracked down Mr. Wilman's retriever?" Bobby lend up on his elbows, excitement growing on his round face.

"A little bit bigger than that case, Bobby. Much bigger!" Hattie beamed.

"Bigger than the kettle mystery? Mrs. Brandon searched everywhere for her iron kettle and we…you found it in Mr. Rollin's yard sale." Amy giggled "He had picked it up with her trash!"

"Compared to this new case friends, the Kettle mystery and the missing dog, was child's play!" Hattie slipped in closer to whisper, so the table next to them couldn't hear as she revealed what it was about.

Bart Brower sat listening at the nearest table and had heard the words, secret and club. It stokes his interest and he wanted to hear more. He motioned for his friends to get quiet and pushed his chair as close as he could without getting caught by Hattie Russel.

"Please tell us Hattie!" Jane Tanner was too excited to finish her desert, so she pushed it aside and lend in closer to her friend. "I'm just nearly busting inside!"

Hattie looked around, noticed Bart Brower had pulled his chair closer to them, so she kept her voice low as she began her story, telling them everything she knew so far.

"Now you know why this is the best mystery that has ever be fall Sleepy Creek!" Hattie looked around at her friend's dropped jaws, eyes wide with uncertainty "Look gang, I need you!"

"And…and you expect us to go up to that…old mansion, alone, at…night!" Amy Collins swallowed at the idea.

"Look, there's going to be a full moon on Christmas Eve and if I can get Mr. Marshall's permission, maybe he will come with us…" Hattie pleated with her frightened friends "and he can unlock the door and go in with us."

"Mr. 'grouch' Marshall, of Marshall Mills!" Bobby Fisher said a bit too loud and some of the students looked their way as Bart Brower nodded his head with a sneaky smile. Knowing he had spoken out, Bobby's round face grew red as he wrinkled his brow. "Sorry Hattie."

"It's alright Bobby, this time, but we better watch those slips." Hattie nodded with her head toward the nosey bully. "Big ears can cause us trouble, if you know what I mean!"

All four club members turn to stare at the nosey boy. Bart tried to force a laugh as he smiled at their leader.

"Got some big secret, Miss Russel?" the bully spit out his words "If you want a club member who's not afraid of their shadow, you best pick me, madam detective!" he laughed, followed by the group of boys sitting with him.

"We can do without your help Bart Brower! Just keep your nose out of our business!" Hattie didn't have any respect for the Brower's, especially this one.

"That suits me, little Miss Russel, the girl with the muscle!" he stood laughing, as he bent over laughing even louder at his lame joke.

"Real cute Bart, the sower tart!" Hattie stood up to leave, tired of this childish game he was playing "Go get your own club started, if you think your smart enough!"

Watching her walk away, he called after her "Come on Hattie, just tell me what your case is about!"

Hattie turned to face him, one last time before leaving the room and spoke out very calmly

"Bart Brower, it's none of your business bee's wax!" her gang walked out laughing, leaving the bully grumbling.

"Just you wait, little smart pants, I'll find out and follow you!"

Hattie opened her bookbag and carefully laid her homework inside, all finished. There were a lot of things to be thankful for during the Christmas season, and Hattie counted less homework a blessing. She glanced up to find her grandmother pulling a big meatloaf out of the oven. Hearing her stomach growl, Hattie looked down at her plate of sampler cookies she had made, trying to find just the right one to call Hattie's Patties. Taking a bite of the first one, Hattie made a face and spit it in a napkin.

"Yuck!" she heard her brother laugh as he walked inside the back door, carrying a basket filled with eggs. Hattie looked up to argue, then spotted the eggs and Matthew's smile "flying chicken feathers!"

"That's right, your majesty! I guess big shot detectives move up the chore latter!" he teased as he walked over to sneak a sample of the good smelling meatloaf.

"Matthew Russel, go wash your hands and stop picking with your little sister!" Nettie walked over to the table with a bowl of green beans and smiled down at the cookies "Haven't found that secret recipe yet child? I had my mother's recipe to go by. Why not borrow my recipe and add some secret ingredients of your own."

"That wouldn't be cheating grandma?" Hattie made a face at her brother when he walked by and pulled her ponytail.

"Not if the owner of the recipe gives it to you dear. Besides the sugar cookie is a simple basic recipe and can be turned into many different kinds." Nettie walked back to get her meatloaf and gravy. "That's how I came up with my chocolate and black walnut cookie."

Hattie got up and tossed the plate of cookies in the trash as John walked in laughing "I hope that trash is buried real deep. Some poor gritter could get a hold of your cookies and die, right there on the spot!" he grabbed his throat as if he were choking "Death from Hattie's Patties!"

"I'll show you John Russel! I'll come up with the best cookie ever created!" she glanced at Nettie "Sorry grandma. Next to your cookies being number one, mine will come in a close second."

"I have all the faith in the world in you, child." Nettie smiled "Hattie's Patties will be the talk of Sleepy Creek."

"Yeh, all the neighbors warning each other to watch out for those poison cookies!" Matthew joined his brother at the table "You should have named them Hattie's killer cookies!"

"Matthew, John, stop picking on your sister at once!" Gideon walked in and gave Hattie a hug "I'll volunteer to be your taste tester Hattie. I married your grandma just for her cookies!"

Joan Byrd

"Old man, go and wash up! See if Carolyn and the other boys are driving in. The biscuits are ready and supper is on the table!"

December 25, 1814 Dear Diary, this has been some Christmas! I opened my gift from Pattie first thing this morning, even before daybreak. I just could not wait another minute. The first thing I laid my eyes on was a gold chest and I just knew there couldn't be stacks of gold lying inside it. It was indeed heavy, so I came to the conclusion that whatever was inside, could not be very heavy after all. My morning eyes were not prepared for what lay inside that chest. It was the most exquisite Christmas dress I have ever seen.

The rich red velvet felt terribly soft to my hand and I was afraid I might make a dent in it if I mashed it too hard. There is the most handsome lace adorning the top and hem. It's snow white with groupings of holly and berries and the biggest white sash and bow my eyes have ever feasted upon. I simply had the need to try it own, right then and there. I could not believe it was me in the mirror. I looked just like a princess Dear Diary, an honest to goodness princess!

Mama was just as surprise as I was when I came down the steps, my hair lying in long ringlets. She told me, I could pass for a Marshall child. Me, a Marshall's child! I could have hugged my dear friend forever, if she had been there!

My happiness was short lived Dear Diary when we walked into church and my dearest friend was nowhere to be seen. She always managed to arrive at church first and save me a seat, but not this Sunday, Christmas Sunday. The church was almost filled up when we arrived, so we had to find seats in the balcony. I guess making over my new dress had thrown us somewhat behind, so I was certain I would be blame for acting so proud.

To my relief, no one in my family blamed me for being late. I think they all could see I was worried about Pattie and I could tell my brother Mark was concerned about Pattie's disappearance too. Mama and daddy tried to reassure me the Marshalls had probably been called away for a family emergency, but I somehow knew, it's was more serious. I can still see that light in the attic and those red eyes staring at me, as if I were to blame for their disappearance.

Then we all went into town for the caroling around the big Christmas tree in the town's square. I just couldn't bring myself to sing. My heart was breaking with sadness, so I wondered away from the group to be alone. That's when I heard Mr. Marshall call out to Pattie. I turned quickly, hoping to see her coming my way but all I saw was Mr. Marshall staring at me, calling me Pattie. Then he began walking toward me swiftly, almost in a run. He was crying uncontrollable as he fell down in front of me and grabbed me tightly into his arms.

Mr. Marshall kept repeating, "Pattie, you're alive! My baby, my little girl! How…did you escape from it? Thank God you are alive! Daddy is so sorry, darling!"

My heart took on a new kind of fear! My best friend could be dead! How? Why? I kept asking myself! Then it dawned on me, the thing at the attic window, something evil and wicked was in Pattie's house! Was that what Mr. Marshall was referring too when he said, how did you escape from it? Suddenly I had to know what happen to Pattie and her daddy obviously knew.

I found the courage to speak to the weeping man. I remember my words clearly and how scared I became when he looked up into my eyes, seeing who I was. I ask him where Pattie was and if she was alright? I told him I was afraid something had happened to her and I begged him to tell me. For a few minutes Mr. Marshall could only stare at me with his cold eyes, then he jumped up and grabbed me angrily. He accused me of stealing his daughters new Christmas dress, said he had just given it to her on the day we came by his office. I finally found my voice and told him of Pattie's visit on the morning of Christmas Eve. Instead of calming down, Mr. Marshall shook me back and forth with force, until I thought my head was going to pop off my neck.

Mr. Marshall became a raving maniac! He slung his head from side to side as though he was looking for a way out and I'm not sure from what, Dear Diary. Something he had done he couldn't take back? Suddenly without warning, he turned and ran to their carriage and climbed onto the empty seat. He released the reigns form their holder and calling wildly to the two horses, drove the carriage down the street and out of sight.

Dear Diary, I just stood there, staring down an empty road, until I felt my daddy lift me up in his strong arms, and without a word, took me home. My heart is broken and I feel real sad. Hattie Russel.

Chapter 9

More clues were springing up for the young detective as she sat in bed contemplating her great-great aunt's last entry from the diary. The Christmas dress Pattie had given her was her very own new one. Why would she give it to her best friend? Did Pattie know she would never wear it because somehow, she knew something bad was about to happen to her. Was Pattie's father somehow involved with her disappearance along with her mother and the entire staff, including the coachman. Hattie had said Mr. Marshall left town on his own. He knew his daughter was in danger from something he had called, It!

Hattie got up, unable to sleep and began pacing the floor as she spoke softly to herself

"If something did happen to Pattie and all the others, then where are their bodies? Are they still somewhere inside that old house?" Hattie scratched her head, trying to make common sense out of it "Hattie stated she had heard someone playing the piano in the Marshall's music room. It would appear Hattie saw the music room on her one visit to the mansion, the evening of the sleep over or the following morning.

Why did Mr. Marshall become so happy on the day they went to his office when just before he was scared of dying and the dark to come?" Hattie looked down at her favorite old doll, as though it could hear her "Mr. Marshall was afraid of something Maggie, but what? Did he know about the thing that lived in the attic? It couldn't have been a ghost, the house was only three years old, according to grandma."

Hearing the grandfather clock down in the hall strike twelve, Hattie knew she must get some sleep, so she wouldn't fall asleep in class. After tossing and turning, Hattie finally fell asleep, only to have her dreams filled with the mystery on the hill.

The Missing Piece Detectives heard all the latest clues from their fearsome leader the next day in the cafeteria and was glad Bart Brower had to stay in class because he didn't do his homework.

The Box in the Attic

Hattie's friends seem to be a little braver about going to the old mansion, but they insisted they take a grown up and not Mr. 'grouch' Marshall.

Hattie pulled her latest batch of cookies from the oven. These, she thought, finally smelled good, so just maybe these would pass grandpa's taste test. After cooling off, she looked at the perfect shape cookie, in the form of two girls in long dresses. Hattie smiled, happy with the way they looked and was proud she had a daddy who could turn her drawing of what her cookie cutter should look like into reality. Adam Russel learned at a young age, watching his father Gideon, how to forge metal in the old farm's forge shop, they called it. The first Russel's used it for making pots, pans, nails, farm brackets, and many other things.

"If these cookies taste as good as they look, I will decorate them with icing. Their long dresses will be Christmas colors and one girl will have blonde hair, the other dark brown, like Aunt Hattie!"

"My goodness child, to icing each cookie by hand will take you a long time." Nettie had been observing her granddaughter ever since she flew through the kitchen door after school, her recipe whirling through her little mind. "Why not just package them as they are Hattie, they're really unique just plain. The factory never icings their cookies and they sale all over the United States."

"Yes grandma, I know. Nettie's cookies are famous just the way they are, but I want my Hattie's Pattie's to be special, just come out for the Christmas Holidays!" Hattie lifted one up and took a big sniff, it was heavenly "So far so good grandma! They look pretty and they smell great!"

"Now the final and most important test, the taste test!" Nettie enjoyed watching her granddaughter interested in cookies, like herself at that age. Then the thought hit her, Hattie's perfect solution for her icing problem "Hattie, since your cookies are just going to be sold at Christmas time, and they're going to be extra special, I purpose you wrapped up one cookie in some of the cookie factory's wrap, and tie a little ribbon around each one, selling it for…$2.00 a piece!"

"Wow! That's a swell ideal grandma!" Hattie looked at the cookie in her hand and took a big breath "Here goes! Wish me luck grandma!" slowly she put the cookie in her mouth and took a small bite. Her eyes lit up with delight and she downed the rest of the great tasting cookie, then licked her lips.

"I take it, they are a success!" Nettie got up and walked over to join the excited girl who was holding out a cookie, just for her approval. If her grandma liked it, she knew she had found her cookie recipe. Without hesitation, Nettie bit into the butterscotch, peanut butter, packed with chocolate chips cookie. Finding the taste remarkably good, Nettie hugged Hattie tightly "Hattie Russel, you have a winner here, young lady! I guarantee you will sale every single cookie you bake!"

"Golly gee, thanks grandma!" Hearing the backdoor open, Hattie saw her grandpa and raced over with one of her Hattie's Patties. "Here you go Grandpa, the best new cookie in Sleepy Creek!"

Gideon Russel winked at his wife of sixty years and took the cookie to examine.

"My Hattie Marie, this here cookie is almost too pretty to eat!" with a twinkle in his brown eyes, he smiled down at the waiting baker. Taking a big bite, he closed his eyes as it melted slowly in his mouth. Matthew and John walked in just in time to see Gideon take the big bite. Matthew punched his brother's arm, pretending to be in a panic.

"John, hurry quickly! Call 911! Grandpa just swallowed some of Hattie's killer cookies!" he snickered as Gideon turned to face the brothers.

"It's too bad you want be getting a taste of these 'wonderful' cookies, boys!" he picked up Hattie and turned her around "Baby girl, you have a great cookie! Real pretty too, to boot!"

"Hattie's aiming on icing them in Christmas colors and selling them in single packages, tied with color ribbon!" Nettie held one up for the boys to see "Hattie's Patties will be the cookie of choice this Christmas, and I dare say, every other Christmas that comes to Sleepy Creek."

Hattie had laid down across her bed on her stomach to read the next entry in Hattie's diary, hoping for more clues. For the last two nights, she had read the book without her grandma present. Nettie had far too much, last minute things to get done before the big open house Saturday afternoon. Hattie was grateful her mother had agreed to let her skip the open house on Saturday so she could accompany her daddy to the holiday market to sale her cookies.

Hattie was happy with the fifty cookies she had baked and decorated, but the process was slow and her time was running out. Matthew and John had promised to take them to the factory and seal them in their own single packages in exchange for one iced cookie. When they ask for another one, she teased them about the possibility of dying after eating two of her 'killer cookies', then she let them take one more a piece for helping her.

"Maggie, I've got two more days left until Saturday and I can get fifty more cookies finished, I'll make two hundred dollars! That will be enough to buy all the Ashton's gifts!" Hattie rubbed the rag doll's head lovingly "Mama called Hilda Ashton and ask her what her three children wanted for Christmas. Now I have a shopping list to go buy. I might need to sale more cookies to get everything they want. Megan is six and she really wants a red bike. Bikes alone can cost lots of money, and she's asked for a few more, small things. Little Charlie, four, wants a red wagon and a big toy truck while little Tess wants a doll that can say mama." Hattie looked down at the diary and said softly "Let's see what Hattie wrote Maggie."

December 26, 1814, Dear Diary, Another Christmas has come and gone and I usually feel let down by its passing. During the season, there is so much going on and all the excitement of the coming activities fill your days with much joy and gladness. Unlike all the other Christmas' in my past, it's not the passing of the season that makes me sad, it's the passing of my dearest best friend, Pattie.

Sitting here tonight, trying to find the words in which to write, I can hardly see to write another word in your beautiful white pages. I felt as though my friend gave me my very own diary to write down all our happy moments together, but it would appear there is only sorrow for my pen to put down. I grow weary of writing when my heart is not in it. With Pattie gone from me forever, I don't know if I shall ever find happiness again.

My first thoughts were to lock you away in that golden chest that Pattie so lovingly gave me and I must admit, Dearest Diary, I almost carried that very plan out until I accidentally dropped the beautiful chest upside down. I was mortified! I just knew I had broken the cherished gift after hearing a strange crack from the inside of the box. To my surprise, when I turned it over and looked inside, I discovered a hidden bottom, deep enough to hold your most priceless treasures! It was empty except for an envelope, addressed to me. I knew right away it was from Pattie! I carefully open the seal, not wanting to destroy anything written from my friend's hand. It was indeed a letter from Pattie and this is her exact words:

"Dear Hattie, I wanted to write you this one last letter to let you know all I know about why I've been acting so weird when we're together. There are strange things going on in this house and I think my father has something to do with it. Up until we went to visit him at his office, my daddy was acting strange, different. Mama had told me about daddy's fears about dying young and the older he became, the quieter he became. Then for some reason, the growing darkness made him afraid, so afraid I would hear him pacing the floor above my room and some nights at midnight, I would find him standing in our rose garden talking to something invisible.

To see daddy so joyful, even singing, on yesterday in his office, I was hoping he had gotten over what had been wrong with him. We had a long chat, like old times, planning what we would be doing as a family on Christmas Eve and Christmas day. Daddy was excited about my Christmas presents and he wanted me to open them when we got home. I've never opened my gifts before Christmas Eve and yet he wanted me to open all but one. He called it my very special Christmas gift that I would have with me forever. For some reason I cannot explain, I felt real scared. Maybe it was the look in daddy's eyes, much different than only moments before. Don't think me mad, dear friend when I tell you, Daddy's look was as if he was not even in his body, like he was somewhere else, far way. It didn't last long and he snapped back into his happy jolly self.

When we arrived home, daddy was very loving to my mama and gave her a beautiful diamond neckless and matching earrings. She was delighted and watched me unwrapped my gifts, the Christmas dress I gave you and the golden chess. He told me he would give me my big special gift on Christmas Eve. I know you must be wondering why I would give you my two gifts dear friend. About the dress, somehow, in my heart, I knew I would never wear that dress for Christmas and what I felt might happen drove me to give you the golden chess as well.

I wrote this letter to you early this morning, Christmas Eve after seeing my daddy slip from the house with some luggage and hide it in the back of the carriage. Hattie, I am scared, really bad. I'm asking you as a friend, if something happens to me, please never stop looking! You must find me, even if it's in Heaven, when your time comes to be welcome by our Lord. Never forget how much I love you. Your friend forever, Pattie Marshall."

Dearest Diary, I will honor my friend's wish and never stop praying for her, I am hoping the wooden cross I put around her neck, helped in some way, to ease what pain she must have in gone though. I will search for Pattie all the days of my earthy life until I see my friend again, in heaven. Hattie Russel

Chapter 10

"Maggie, this case gets more and more confusing! Why didn't Pattie share what she was afraid of? Maybe she wasn't really sure but she felt like something was in the mansion. It makes sense why Pattie became afraid of her daddy. One might understand his fear of dying, due to his own father and grandfather dying in their early fifties, but his sudden fear of night time and talking with an invisible thing in the rose garden and twelve midnight. Hum, you know Maggie, that's what some folks call the bewitching hour. You don't suppose Mr. Marshall was talking to the devil and making some sort of deal with him? Gosh! This could get really scary Maggie if Lucifer is involved somehow!"

Hattie walked over to the window and looked out at the clear night sky. The moon was just beginning its new moon and by Christmas Eve, it would be completely full, just like it was two hundred years ago.

"That thing Hattie witness in the attic appeared to be some sort of being with red eyes!" she walked over to her bed and climbed under the covers, feeling a chill. "Maggie, I must stay brave! I will not let the evil devil keep me from finding out what happen to Pattie and all those other people! If I tell my friends the devil may be what's up in that attic or one of his demons, I can bet all three will chicken out of going inside that old mansion."

Hattie picked up her doll and hugged it in her arms "Maggie, If I have to go inside that old house all by myself, I will! Aunt Hattie is counting on me! I won't let her down!"

Saturday morning came in cloudy, with a chance of snow before night fall, so the market square should be busting with Christmas' shoppers. Hattie had managed to finish two hundred cookies with help from her three friends and grandma. Now she would be making $400, if she could sale every single Hattie's Patties. So, her hopes were up when she set up her little booth next to her father's large booth. Hattie had made a large sign explaining what she would be doing from the sales that read: All MONEY RECEIVED WILL BE

The Box in the Attic

GOING TO CHRISTMAS GIFTS FOR THE ASHTON FAMILY. $2.00 each!

Hattie had placed several Hattie's Patties in a pretty Christmas basket, others were laid around on her white table cloth. Adam Russel had made her a tin box with an opening in the top to slide the money in. Hattie had barely sat down when her first customer stepped up and picked up one of the beautiful cookies.

"Hattie Russel, this is a very pretty Christmas cookie if I ever saw one!" June and her sister Tracy smiled down at the young girl "Did you get your grandmother to help you come up with it?"

"No ma'am, this is my very own recipe Miss Farrell! It not only looks pretty, it tasted even better!" Hattie smiled at the owners of Sleepy Creek Café and Bakery "I bet your shop has been doing a great business this season. I've never seen a better crowd for the festival."

"My yes child, we've been buzzing with customers!" the friendly woman pulled out her wallet "We had to hire extra help this year so it aloud Tracy and myself a little time to come to the market for a few things to use in the café."

Tracy Farrell read the sign and smiled broadly "Sister, this child is doing the work of the Lord! So thoughtful to think of others in their time of need. I say we buy twenty cookies to share with our workers and if they taste as good as they look, we might ask you to bake us some to sale in the bakery."

"That is a wonderful ideal Tracy!" June's gaze fell on Hattie "You would have time I hope? We would give you two dollars, just like you're asking and we can easily get three and make a dollar profit." She pulled out a fifty-dollar bill and slid it in the tin box. "A little something extra to help with your cause. God bless you child." Taking the bag of cookies, the Farrell sister walked on over to the Russel Farm stand. When Hattie looked up, she had a line of customers.

At twelve noon, Adam walked over smiling at his little girl who had sold all but one hundred cookies. "Hattie, we still have three hours to go and looks like you are going to sale out way before then."

"I hope so daddy! Some of my customers have put in a little extra to help the Ashton's"

"That's terrific Hattie! You can buy that family everything they

Joan Byrd

wished for and more. It's time for lunch! We close the booth and go to the café. Get your things and let's go."

"Daddy, could you bring me back a sandwich and hot chocolate! I think I'll stay and sale cookies. I see new people coming in the square. Please!" Hattie looked up, her big brown eyes pleading.

"Okay, if you're sure you are not getting to cold out here." Her daddy smiled at the excited girl.

"No daddy, I wrapped up really good this morning." Hattie smiled "Don't worry, I'll be fine."

"Alright Hattie, but if you change your mind, we'll be right over there." He nodded toward the café, then joined his father and James and Thomas, who had come to help in the farm booth.

Hattie had made several sales and was bending down to get the last fifty cookies when her eyes were drawn to very black shiny boots. Slowly she moved up the body, black pants and a long black wool overcoat. When Hattie sit up and gazed into the man's dark eyes, she shuddered. His stare made her suddenly feel cold. Only moments before, she bravely called out to passing visitors, "Hattie's Patties! Special Christmas cookies, two dollars each!" now she had a hard time speaking without stuttering.

"May…I…help…you…sir?" he continued to stare, not blinking his eyes. "Would you…like to buy a cookie? It's for a really good cause."

"What cause?" the tall man's voice came out low and deep "Your piggy bank perhaps?"

Making Hattie mad, she stood straight and looked back at the stranger "It is not for my piggy bank mister! It is to buy Christmas Presents for the Ashton family! They have three little children, Megan, six, Charlie, four and little Tess, age two! Their daddy, Drake Ashton was fired from his job at the Marshall Mill because he couldn't make it to work!"

"Then he should have gotten fired!" the stranger remained cold "You cannot expect an employer to keep a lazy person on their payroll, young lady!"

"Begging your pardon sir, Drake Ashton is not a lazy man, he fell at work from a rotten latter and broke both his legs! The man was only carrying out orders from his foreman!" Hattie placed her hands on her hips, angry at this seemingly uncaring man "The owner

50

of Marshall Mills had no cause in firing that poor man! If you ask me, he's just plain mean!"

"Mean, is he?" a slight grin fell on his lips "You, madam, are a very out spoken young woman! You look a great deal like someone I use to know." His eyes became serious again "What is your name child?"

"Hattie Russel!" she waited a moment "It's polite to exchange names sir, what your name." she noticed his eyes had grown wider. She swallowed before asking again "Your name sir?"

"Your cookies, you called them Hattie's Patties. Why such an unusual name and" He looked down for the first time at the cookie shape like two girls, hugged up. "I see two girls hugging one another, like friends."

"I named my cookies after two very close friends, if you must know sir. My great-great aunt Hattie, whom I'm named after, and her dearest friend in the entire world, Pattie Marshall." Hattie watch the stranger slowly pick up one of the cookies "Would you like to buy one? They're very good."

"Pattie Marshall?" Hattie noticed a tear run down the man's cheek, maybe he had a heart, she thought, hidden somewhere inside that cold body. "Pattie." His voice was soft as he continued to stare at the cookie. "I'll take this one." He pulled out a wallet and instantly Hattie noticed the large amount of cash he had inside it. He looked up and caught her looking. She looked away quickly as he pulled out a bill and place it in the tin box. Placing the cookie in his coat pocket, the stranger reached over and patted Hattie's head.

"You are a sweet girl to help this family, Hattie Russel. Sweetness must run in your family." She looked up to see him smiling at her "Maybe there will be a brighter day for Drake Ashton when he gets well. You may give him another gift from me, telling him William Marshall has given him his job back."

"William Marshall? You're...Mr. Marshall?" Hattie's eyes were as wide as his smile.

"The mean old boss? The one in the same my new friend." He winked "Good luck with your sales Hattie!" he turned and started to walk away, then looked back speaking softly, just for her ears "Ashton's doctor bills will be paid too Hattie Russel! Merry Christmas!" he walked away as she called after him.

"Merry Christmas to you William, and God bless you!" Hattie

noticed he stopped for a brief moment, as though the last words she had spoken meant something, then he waved and kept walking down the street until he was out of sight.

Hattie hadn't noticed the crowd gathering around whispering and it dawned on her how quiet everyone had become when Mr. Marshall walked up, all though she knew they could not have heard what he was saying to her. Hearing a woman's voice across the street from the town square, Hattie saw Libby Fisher walking directly toward her. She jumped when she felt the hand on her shoulder and looked up into her daddy's warm eyes.

"Didn't mean to scare you darling, I brought your lunch." Noticing the whispering crowd and the bookworm running across the street, Adam Russel suddenly wondered what excitement he had missed. "Hattie, did something just happen out here?"

"Yes daddy, you won't believe it! I sold a cookie to" before Hattie could finish her sentence, Libby Fisher had reached the booth, eyes wide in unbelief.

"I saw it for myself and I still can't believe it!" Libby Fisher stared down at the young girl.

"Would you care to fill me in on what you are talking about Libby?" Adam couldn't understand why a single customer buying one of his daughter's cookie was causing such a commotion.

"Adam Russel, your daughter had a very long conversation with none other than William Franklin Marshall! Standing right here in this very spot!" the outspoken woman still couldn't believe it.

"The William Franklin Marshall?" Adam looked down at his daughter in amazement "Hattie, what on earth did the two of you talk about, surely not your cookies?"

"Why daddy, William was asking me lots of questions about my cookies as well as other things." Hattie smiled up at the wide-eyed book store owner "Do you know what else he did, he gave Mr. Ashton his job back and is going to take care of all his doctor's bill. I think Mr. Marshall is a very nice man under that grumpy exterior."

"A nice man? Don't believe everything you hear Hattie Russel!" Libby Fisher turned up her nose and started to walk away when Hattie called after her.

"At least Mr. Marshall bought one of my cookies Mrs. Fisher!" Hattie gave the woman her biggest smile when she turned around "Would you like to buy one? Your son helped me paint the icing on."

"Why, of course child." Libby blushed as she heard Adam Russel chuckle "I'll take three. Bobby did tell me they taste very good." She pulled out her six dollars then looked down at the money box "You can slide this in on top of Marshall's two dollars, if he didn't put in play money."

"I can prove Mr. Marshall is a man of his word, Mrs. Fisher, right now!" Hattie opened her box, expecting to see his two dollars and a gasp came from the three watching at the sight of a new one-hundred-dollar bill.

Chapter 11

All the Russel's had gathered in their big den to discuss the holiday games that would be taking place the following night in the town square. The family had always competed in the skating races, the ice rope- pull and the downhill sledding. Their biggest opponents were the Brower family, who were always bragging they would win every game and up until this year, it had been an even split. The skating races had always been won by the Russel's, while the Brower's always managed to win the downhill sledding by cutting their opponents off and causing them to crash. The ice rope pull had been won by the Russel's up until last year when the Brower's talked the judges into letting them wear new gloves that had gripers on the palm side.

"With these new gloves fellows, we're back on top!" Andrew checked out his warm gloves with gripers built in for sure grip. "At least the Brower's can't cheat this year, we'll be even!"

"Hattie, do you think you can take on Bart this year in one of the games?" Peter reached over and rubbed his sister's head "I heard him bragging down at the cookie factory this morning about being in the big games this year and to quote the little jerk, 'I'm gonna beat the crap out of any Russel against me!"

"That's Bart alright, always bragging!" Hattie smiled at her brothers "I may be a girl but I know how to skate and go sledding! I know I can whip Bart Brower at anything, even rope pulling!"

"That's a pretty rough sport little girl." Matthew tried to picture their sister helping them at rope pull. "You might just get in our way when we start sliding back and forth."

"Look fellows, Hattie is one of us and I say if Shannon can do it, so can Hattie, even though she's six years younger than the delightful Shannon Brower." James made a face "We can put her up front, were it's safer."

"Boys, I'm not sure about that arrangement." Carolyn had been reading and had overheard her children "If the Brower's win, that means Hattie will be the first to fall in the broken ice, right in the frigid cold water. She'll catch her death of a cold and there goes her Christmas."

The Box in the Attic

"Hey mama, where is your confidence in our boys?" Adam winked at his daughter "I just happen to believe our family will beat those Brower's in all three games!"

"I agree with your daddy kids! Those Brower's need to be shown a thing or two and now that Hattie makes our team complete, we've got a fighting chance." Gideon stood up to put another log on the fire.

"Hattie did what everyone in Sleepy Creek thought was impossible, she made friends with Mr. Marshall."

"If anyone can bring the good out of a soul, it's Hattie Russel!" Nettie lifted up her new sweater she had been knitting to have a look. "That one is finished for Megan Ashton! Two more to go and the entire family will be sporting new Nettie's originals."

"It's very pretty grandma!" Hattie stood up and stretched, wanting to be excused to go read the next entry in Aunt Hattie's diary "As for my new friend William, I think he's just a lonely man who acts years older than he really is. He's really quite handsome when he smiles."

"Are you telling us Mr. Marshall actually smiled at you child?" Gideon walked over beside his granddaughter and touched her face. "I'd say you worked a Christmas miracle."

"And I believe Mr. Marshall was touched by the heart of a child and it melted his cold as ice attitude, at least for our Hattie." Adam winked at his daughter "With his $100 donation, she made $650 dollars from her Hattie's Patties to buy presents for the Ashton family."

"Hey little sister, you might have some left over to buy me a better gift this year!" Matthew teased.

"Very funny Matthew!" Hattie walked toward the stairs "You'll get a nice gift, but it won't come out of this money. Every single penny will go to help that dear family."

"We're really proud of you sis." Andrew walked over and hugged her "And as the oldest, I welcome you to the Russel team for this year's holiday games!"

"Thanks Andrew! I won't let you or our team down and we will beat those Brower's this year!" Hattie returned her brother's hug and walked up to her room to read.

December 27, 1814, Dear Diary, today we took out the dried-up Christmas tree and I felt as dead inside as it appeared on the outside. I hadn't noticed the. single present that had been left under the tree until my daddy lifted the old tree up to carry it away. The pretty red paper and crisps white bow looked as pretty as the day I wrapped it up for my dear friend. I lifted it off the cold floor, ever so gently and carried it up to my room. I did not have the heart to unwrap it because it belonged to Pattie and in my heart, I hoped one day I could give it to her, somewhere, someway.

I did not have to look inside to know what I had made for her. I could see it in my mind, just as clear as the day I laid the framed painting inside the cardboard box. I was amazed at how much the painting resembled me and Pattie, just like I was looking in a mirror and we were smiling back, arms around one another. Knowing I would never forget what my friend's face looked like, I hide the present inside the hidden bottom of the gold chest until the day that someone might find it and deliver the gift, from my heart, to my dearest friend.

Mama and I went into town today to buy a few supplies at Freeman's store and I persuaded her to walk with me to Mr. Marshall's office. I was in hopes that Pattie's daddy would be there but everything was dark inside the rock building and there was a sign posted on the door stating: William F. Marshall is not here and he will not be here in the for-see-able future. Please contact Harvey Patterson for any business you might have pertaining to Marshall Mills.

Mr. Marshall was gone, Pattie was gone and everyone who lived inside the Marshall mansion. It's hard to think they're all gone, simply vanished. I can still see each of their faces, all happy and excited about the coming of Christmas. Mrs. Folly, a very jolly woman whose fat tummy shook when she laughed at the butler's funny jokes. The distinguished man who had a British accent, Mr. Rockford was always the polite butler and Milly and Tilly Shields, were twin sisters who got the jobs as chamber maids. The personal maids were always at hand to help whenever anyone in the family needed anything. Rose was Mrs. Marshall's personal maid, Velda helped William Marshall and Pattie's extra sweet maid was Joyce Ann. All lovely people. Mr. Peppers was the gardener and was kind enough to take me out to the rose garden and show me the statue of the virgin Mary. She was as tall as Pattie's mama and I thought she was very beautiful standing in the middle of what I knew must be lovely roses when in bloom. The coachman, Mr. Torrance was very kind to me as well, he always had nice things to say about the people living in Sleepy Creek. It's hard to think of them without crying, knowing I might never see any of them ever again, especially Pattie.

I just cannot write another word Dear Diary. My eyes are blurred with tears, so I must close for this night. Hattie Russel

"Galloping grasshoppers! Gosh Maggie, the painting is inside that chest! It's been there all this time, unless Aunt Hattie took it out when she got older and wanted to see it again!" Hattie got down and pulled the gold chest out from under her bed. Carefully opening the lid, she took the stack of drawings out and stared down at the bottom, trying to find a tab to pull up. "It's got to be here somewhere Maggie!" Hattie ran her fingers slowly around the outside of the fake bottom. "Aunt Hattie found it when she accidentally dropped it, but it's much older now and could possibly break if I try that."

Picking up the chest, Hattie gave it a little shake, hoping to hear the present rattle inside. No sound came from the chest and Hattie picked up her doll as she pondered what to do next.

"Maggie, the chest is either empty now or the painting is the exact size of the chest and it's fitting inside real snug." Hattie sat her doll on the rim of the chest and began pacing the floor. She twirled back around when she heard a loud click. Looking down in the chest she saw her doll lying in the bottom where she had fallen and hit the secret button. "Maggie, you found it!" she lifted her favorite doll out and sat her on the bed. Slowly, Hattie opened the secret door and saw red paper and a mashed white bow, Hattie's gift to Pattie.

"Here it is grandma, the painting Aunt Hattie wrapped for her best friend two hundred years ago!" Hattie had called her grandmother as she was going in to her bedroom for the night and said she had something to show her. Nettie lifted the present and admired the perfect wrapping.

"I see you haven't opened it dear. Aren't you curious to see what they looked like?" Nettie laid the delicate gift back on Hattie's bed. "We were always told that Aunt Hattie had dark brown hair and brown eyes, just like you child, and that her friend Pattie had long blonde hair and blue eyes. The stories past down tells us how close they were and how your aunt Hattie never got over her friend's disappearance till the day she died."

"I can hear that closeness when I read Aunt Hattie's diary and how heartbroken she was at the sudden loss of her very best friend." Hattie laid the gift back inside the chest along with the drawings, then closed the lid. "I won't open Hattie's special gift to Pattie, grandma. Aunt Hattie's wish was that whoever found the gift should give it to her friend Pattie, so she could open her long- awaited present from her dear friend."

"Hattie, Pattie will never see that special loving gift. Two hundred years have passed and unless there is a ghost inside that old house to give it to, that two- hundred- year old Christmas gift will remain tucked away in that chest forever." Nettie patted her granddaughter on the head and walked over to the door "Let me know when you give up searching for someone long gone Hattie and we'll see that lovely painting together."

Chapter 12

Hattie felt somewhat let down by her grandma's words as she climbed under the covers and pulled her doll in her arms.

"Maggie, I can understand why grandma told me I couldn't ever give Pattie her Christmas gift from Aunt Hattie. I'm old enough to know a person wouldn't still be alive after two-hundred-years but that doesn't mean their wondering spirit can't be trapped inside that old mansion! Pattie wrote in the letter she had hidden that her daddy told her the surprise gift from him would be with her forever. On Christmas Eve there was a full moon when Pattie opened the special gift and when Aunt Hattie came knocking, she found all the shutters closed and locked from inside." Hattie's mind was filled with too many questions to fall asleep so she got up and walked over to peek out at the moon.

"Just suppose that gift was something evil and when Pattie opened it...the horrible thing Aunt Hattie saw in the attic, was a demon and...he locked them inside to torment them, forever!"

Friday night turned out to be partly cloudy, so the moon was made visible whenever the clouds moved from in front of it's bright glow. The Russel children had put on their warmest clothes for the winter games and just the excitement of whooping the Brower bunch made their blood feel a lot warmer.

Hattie looked over the crowd gathered to witness the competing teams and wondered if William Marshall had come out. To her disappointment, she didn't see her new friend. Feeling a hard punch on her arm, Hattie turned to face Bart Brower's cocky grin.

"Little Miss Muscle Russel, get ready to be blasted!" he sneered.

"Keep dreaming Brower! Just keep out of my way and I'll show you how a real- athletic wins!" Hattie watched as the bullies sixteen-year-old sister walked over and grabbed his arm and pulled him over to their family. Shannon Brower turned back to look at the young girl, then her gaze went to Andrew for a few seconds until her older brother tuned her around to give them orders.

Andrew waved his team in a circle for a final pep talk before the skating races began where half their group would compete.

"Alright, the four oldest will go first! Keep your eyes on the Brower's, especially Randy, James. He tripped you up last year and you almost didn't get in on time!"

"I'm ready for the little cheat, brother!" James fastened on his ice skates and winked at his little sister "You cheer for us real loud Hattie!"

"I'll be the loudest cheerleader out here James! You can count on me!" Hattie hugged her four brothers for luck "Now go skate circles around those bragging Brower's!"

"You got it little sis!" Andrew moved out to the ice rink and whispered to the other three "Let's whip butt, boys!"

The boys were in their places when the town's mayor pulled out his whistle and blew it loudly, starting the ten- round course. The Brower's went out fast, which brought smiles to the Russel's, knowing that was the reason they always lost the race. The bullies would be well spent around the eighth round, making room for the Russel boys to sail around them to victory.

As promised, James stayed clear of his ravel and the four brothers were welcomed with loud cheers at the finish line.

"First game down, two to go!" Andrew spoke out of breath as he smiled down at his sister "Are you ready to whip Bart Brower kid?"

"Aye-aye captain!' Hattie gave her team leader a salute and her winning smile "Bart the Tart won't know what wheezed past him on the hill!"

"Good to hear that confidence coming from our newest team member!" Andrew gave his sister a wink, then turned his attention on John, Matthew, and Thomas. "Alright, fellows, let those sleds fly down that slope and remember Shannon Brower is a young lady, so act like gentleman!" Andrew walked them over to the high hill overlooking the park "I'll be waiting at the bottom to congratulate you!"

On their way up the deep slope, the three brothers warned Hattie about the curves where the Brower's tried to wreak them with their sneaky move.

"When you near the curves, hang back enough that the Brower closest to you will get around it first, then take him or her, on the downhill, understand?" Matthew took a deep breath when he reached the top "Let's win this year and show those jerks!"

They could hear the mayor talking over a loud mic from speakers placed on top of the hill.

"Alright, teams, remember no pushing or tripping when descending the hill! You must be on your best behavior because we cannot see everything from down below!"

John bent over next to his family "Our very polite adversary will listen to every single one of those rules, I bet!" Laughing, Matthew whispered

"I'm sure they let it go in one ear and out the other!" he took his place on his sled and listened for the whistle. When it came, the sleds flew down the lighted hill.

The race was very close and Hattie spotted a curve ahead and Bart's rolling his eyes over at her. Knowing his bad intention, Hattie hung back causing Bart to turn his head around and lose control of his sled. Hattie saw him heading straight for a big tree and she yelled out for him to look out. The scared boy jerked away just before slamming head on into the deadly tree and he flipped over and watched Hattie sled past him.

Just ahead Hattie could make out Thomas and Bradley Brower in a close race down the hill. Suddenly Bradley slid his sled sideways aiming for Thomas's sled, when out of the blue, Shannon guided her sled over next to her brothers and bumped him out of Thomas's way, letting Thomas go past safely. It appeared to Hattie, that Shannon was fussing at her younger brother, then the young woman turned and moved swiftly down the last steep grade, reaching the finish line behind Matthew, John, and Thomas. Hattie knew if she got in before the other Brower boys, her team would win.

Seeing the final curve ahead, Hattie slowed down to make sure Harold Brower wasn't waiting for her. She could hear a sled coming swiftly behind her and she assumed it was Bradley and not seeing the other Brower brother, Hattie speeded toward the curve and just as she started around the curve, Harold slid into her sideways, were he had been hiding, waiting on her. Losing control, Hattie flipped over as the two- brothers raced past her laughing. Hattie got back on her sled and headed down, knowing she had let her team down when she heard Mayor Sharp's whistle, announcing time was up.

The Russel's had come close but it would be called a tie.

"Hattie, you mustn't blame yourself." Andrew hugged his sad sister "If they knew how the Brower's are always cheating on that hill, they wouldn't let them race!"

"They're not all bad Andrew." Hattie's attention fell on Shannon, who was looking down disappointed. Hattie wondered if the Brower girl was disappointed because it was a tie or because her brothers cheated. Hattie had witness her helping Thomas when her brother Bradley tried to wreak him.

"I don't get what you mean Hattie?" Andrew looked down at his sister "Did you hit your head up there when you flipped over?"

"I did not!" Hattie placed her hands on her hips "I saw Shannon stop her brother Bradley from wreaking Thomas! Isn't that right Thomas?"

"Dang sis, it happened so fast, I can't recollect what happen up there!" Thomas was still obviously shaken up from the near accident.

"Well I saw the whole thing and she not only saved your butt, she gave Bradley a piece of her mind!" Hattie watched Andrew look her way and could tell his and Shannon's eyes locked for a moment before he rubbed the top of his sister's head. "Let's pull some Brower's in the ice water!"

Eight on one side, eight on the other and a large whole between them filled with frigid water. The iced rope game was about to begin and at the sound of the whistle, the pulling started. It went back and forth for almost ten minutes and each side was growing weary. Bart and Hattie were out front and his eyes kept baring into hers with hate. She thought as she tugged the slick rope

"Bart Brower, you, ungrateful bully! I save your butt on that hill and that's the thanks I get!"

"Pull harder gang, they're getting weaker!" Andrew cheered on his team as Matthew blew out his breath.

"They're not the only ones, big brother!"

"I know that stupid, just make them think we have more energy!" Andrew grunted as he pulled.

"I feel fresh as a daisy!" Hattie called out loudly "This is loads of fun guys! I think I could do this all night!

The brothers knew what Hattie was doing and decided they

would use a little reverse psychiatry on their competitors.

"I've only began to fight! I think that extra bowl of spinach gave me a lot of energy tonight!" Matthew laughed out loud "Move over Popeye, there's a new man in town!"

"Hey little brother, I think you're right!" Andrew called out from the rear. "It was great going down and it's even better coming out in our muscles!"

Bart was the first to let go of the rope which caused the others to start sliding forward, pushing the younger brother into the ice water. The game was over, The Russel's had won two out of three games, tying the third.

Mayor Sharp started to hand out the trophies, two first place trophies for the Russel's and two trophies for making a tie. Before he could hand out the last two tied trophies, a strong deep voice came from the crowd.

"Stop right there, Sharp! That should be another first-place trophy for the Russel children!"

The big group of spectators grew silent when the tall dark figure walked out of the shadows "Miss Russel would have gotten down that hill if the Brower boy had not wreaked her sled! I witness the entire race from my hiding place in the woods." William Franklin Marshall walked up to the nervous mayor as the owner of Marshall Mills continued by pointing to the dripping wet boy, wrapped in a warm blanket.

"That boy tried to crash Hattie first around the first curve and he almost ran himself into a big oak before she yelled for him to watch out!" Marshall's eyes burned down on the Brower brothers "This lot has been cheating up on that hill for some time! It's time the real winners receive all three trophies!"

Taking the third first place reward in his hand, William Marshall walked over to Hattie and handed it to her, then smiled.

"This is rightfully yours, my friend, you earned it!" The town citizens and visitors watched in stun silence as the richest man in Sleepy Creek stood over the Russel child. They held their breath as he bent down and lifted her into his arms to give her a hug. "I'm very proud of you Hattie. I hope to see you again soon."

William Marshall lowered Hattie to the frozen ground and patted her head as she smiled up warmly.

"Thank you, William, I would like that very much." Hattie,

along with the large crowd watched the tall private gentleman walk back in the shadows and disappear.

"Did you see that?" Libby Fisher spoke out "I cannot believe that man taking interest in the Russel child! He must be up to something! He never shows his face in public and it obvious he doesn't care to socialize with the people of Sleepy Creek!"

"Speaking of his face, did any of you get a good look at him?" June Farrell stepped up next to Mrs. Fisher "I was on the town's welcoming committee when Mr. Marshall first came to Sleepy Creek, some years back. I swear, that man has not aged a day since then."

"Come to think of it sister, you are exactly right!" Tracy Tanner shook her head "The man is as handsome as ever, and that's the gospel truth!"

"Face lift, I grant you!" Libby Fisher snapped "The man is loaded with money, he stays locked away inside that old stone house, so it would be quite simple for him to get an outside Plastic Surgeon to move in for a while and fix him up!" she snickered.

"I beg your pardon Mrs. Fisher, I think William Marshall did no such thing!" Hattie took up for her new friend "I believe if 'Christian' people would stop gossiping about the poor man and show him a little more respect and Christ like love, he would start treating everyone different!"

"What would a child know?" the book worm felt her face flushing from the stares she was receiving "I consider myself a good Christian woman Hattie Russel and I know when someone is a heathen! The man has never seen the inside of a church! What does he know about love?"

"I could ask you the same question ma'am, but I see how you love Bobby." Hattie kept her voice calm and polite "Mr. Marshall has shown me love and I love him too! I guess he chooses his friends carefully Mrs. Fisher, so I wouldn't be worrying about him bothering you." Hattie turned and walked away as her grandpa Gideon smiled at the frowning woman and chuckled.

"Libby Fisher, sometimes the truth comes out of the mouths of babes. It would do some of us good to listen and learn." He tilted his head to the big- eyed woman "See you at church Mrs. Fisher." Gideon left with his family as Bobby Fisher took his mother's hand and pulled her home.

Chapter 13

"Maggie, the diary doesn't give me any more clues about the mystery." Hattie closed the book and pulled it close to her "Aunt Hattie always mentions missing Pattie in each of her entries, even the last one." Her brown eyes fell on her doll "I skipped over to the last page for now Maggie. She wrote that she knew her days were growing short and soon she would be in heaven with all her loved ones, including her dearest friend Pattie. She said that maybe Pattie could tell her what happen to her on Christmas Eve, 1814 but she thought in heaven, all bad things were wiped from our memories, and she said that would be fine as long as they were together again." Hattie walked over and gazed out at the moon.

"It's almost full Maggie! Aunt Hattie said she had just turned ninety, so I reckon she passed away right after her last entry, May 12, 1894." She continued to stare at the moon as she thought "I just can't picture Aunt Hattie as an old woman but as the young ten-year-old in 1814, hugged up with Pattie, before she vanished."

Hattie walked over and climbed in the bed and switched the lamp out as she pondered what her next move would be.

"Maggie, Christmas Eve is a week away. I guess it's time I pay my friend William a visit. I've got to come up with a plan to go into town all by myself and I think I know how!"

"Grandma, I need to go Christmas shopping today and get those gifts for the Ashton's and all of yours. I'd rather not have you see what I buy everyone, so it will be a surprise." She washed the breakfast dishes, trying hard not to sound too anxious. "Bobby, Jane and Amy said they were free to help me and I could come back home with daddy and grandpa when they're finished at the market."

"How are you planning on getting to town sweetheart? Your daddy left right after breakfast and your mama and the boys left at five this morning. It's the factories biggest week in cookie sales." Nettie dried the last plate and put it in the cabinet before looking down at her granddaughter. "Have you got a ride?"

"Oh yes grandma, the Farrell sisters said they would give me a lift when they come by to get those Hattie's Patties I baked for them." Hattie hung up her apron and smiled her brightest smile "They said they would be more than glad to take me. Aren't they wonderful? Daddy said he had plenty of room for the bike and other presents on the big wagon!" she laughed "He goes to town with a full load and comes home with just money from all the sales!"

"Then you better run up and get your things before the Farrell sisters get here." Nettie watched her granddaughter race upstairs and called after her "I'll keep a look out for June and Tracy."

"Thanks grandma!" Hattie called down, happy everything was working out the way she had planned it "I've got a full day ahead, but I can't wait to check off my list!" Hattie looked in the mirror and whispered, "And pay my friend William a visit and see what he can tell me about the Marshall mystery!"

After getting paid for the fifty cookies from the Farrell sisters, Hattie sat out for the hardware store for her first gifts. The owner, Mickie Freeman, helped her pick out a bike for Megan, then quickly lowered the sale, stating it was his way he could help the Ashton's. He also gave Hattie a good sale on Mr. Ashton's gift, along with her gifts to her father, grandfather, and seven brothers. After agreeing to wrap them all up, except the red bike which would be sporting a giant white bow, Mr. Freedom promised to deliver her order to Adam Russel's farm stand on the town square.

"Thank you, Mickie, and God bless you for the goodness shown the Ashton family as well as mine." Hattie handed him the gift cards, filled out with the recipient of each present and who it was from. "If that's all you need from me, I'm off to the mill store to buy for the women on my list! See you at church." He smiled and patted her head as he opened the store door for her.

"Good luck on your shopping Hattie!"

"I'll have the blue blanket for my grandma, and the white one for my mama." Hattie pulled out her wallet.

"Dear, we will be glad to give you these items half price, but I'm afraid the two blankets and the warm wool coat for Hilda Ashton will still be over your budget." The salesclerk felt bad, knowing she had to follow company policy never to go under half price during Christmas. "Last year your allowance allowed you to get your mama, grandma, and two best friends some woolen gloves, a much smaller item."

The Box in the Attic

"Things are different this year Miss Gram. I talked my brothers into going in together, so we could buy our parents and grandparents something real nice this Christmas. They thought it was a wonderful ideal, especially knowing I would be getting them off the hook to go shopping." Hattie smiled "Hilda's present will come from my cookie sale."

"Hattie Russel, you are an example for the rest of Sleepy Creek to live by." Miss Gram walked over to the latest young girl's pajama fashion and pulled down two small sizes. "You may give these to your friends Jane and Amy, compliments from Marshall Mills!"

"Why, thank you Miss Gram, but, aren't you afraid you'll get in trouble with your boss?" Hattie knew she had to buy her three friends something nice, but nothing as expensive as the flannel pajamas.

"I shall not be getting into any trouble Hattie!" The friendly lady pulled down a roll of pretty Christmas paper and started wrapping the first gift. "This will be my way of helping this year and I can pay for them with my store discount."

"But I can't expect you to pay for them, Miss Gram." Hattie couldn't get over the generosity of Miss Gram and Mr. Freeman, from the hardware store.

"I can and I will! Now stop all that fretting Hattie and finish filling out those gift cards." The salesclerk placed a green ribbon around the pretty paper and tied a beautiful big bow right on top. "Now, just lay your money on the counter and go about your shopping. I'll see that your packages will be delivered to your father's stand this afternoon."

After thanking the woman again, Hattie made her way to the toy shop where she bought the red wagon, big truck, talking doll and several other gifts for the three Ashton children. They would be wrapped and delivered to Adam Russel before he left for home, so Hattie skipped to the bookstore and scanned the row of youth books and picked out six more Nancy Drew books for herself, a gift from her grandma Nettie. One last stop to make before going to visit her friend, William Marshall. Bobby Fisher loved to play the games at the local game shop, so with the extra money she had left from not having to spend it on her two girlfriends, Hattie bought him a twenty- dollar gift card and had it wrapped in a small box. Her

67

shopping was finished and she found herself standing right outside the stone house at the end of town.

Hattie knocked on the big wooden door and stood back when she heard heavy footsteps. Opening back the door, an unsmiling, heavy set man stared down at her, his serious expression made her step back even further. He tilted his head as he spoke

"Can I help you, little girl? Are you here to sale something?" the butler continued, not giving her a chance to respond, "A little late in the season to be selling girl scout cookies, isn't it miss?"

"Begging your pardon sir, the reason for my visit is not to sale cookies. I sold my cookies down at the town's square last Saturday." Hattie put on her special smile at the stone face standing over her "My family is known for their famous cookies sir. Maybe you've heard of them, Nettie's Cookies?"

"Nettie's cookies? Indeed, they are quite tasty." The robust man narrowed his eyes "Your cookie wouldn't be called, Hattie's Patties, would they?"

"The same!" she thrust out her hand "Hattie Russel, here to see my good friend, William Marshall!"

"Theodore, for God's sake, my good sir, let the lady in." William Marshall had overheard the conversation between his young friend and his loyal butler of sixty years, Theodore Johnson, who had accompanied him from Boston, Mass. Thirty years ago.

Stepping inside the cozy little stone cottage, Hattie felt the warmth coming from a huge stone fireplace and saw her friend William standing next to the hearth, smiling.

"Come on in Hattie and joined me in some hot chocolate." He glanced over at his butler, who was obviously confused.

"Not your usual hot tea sir? 'Hot chocolate?" the butler stood, waiting for the possible correction.

"No tea this time Theodore. I think my young friend would prefer a nice cup of hot chocolate, topped with marshmallows." William Marshall smiled down at Hattie "What do you say Hattie Russel?"

"I simply love hot chocolate William, even more so with lots of marshmallows!" Hattie's eyes lit up, then she heard the heavy butler grunt "Unless, of course, you prefer hot tea. I must admit, I've never tried it, so with lots of cream and sugar added, I could give it a whirl."

Mr. Marshall laughed softly and motioned his loyal worker away "Hot chocolate for my friend, Theodore, extra marshmallows, and I will have the same." He helped Hattie out of her coat and offered her a seat. "So, what brings you to town today Hattie, besides this lovely visit?"

"Christmas shopping! I had a lot of gifts to buy and I was running out of time." Hattie looked around the sitting room, lit only by lamps. Her attention was drawn to the painting over the huge mantle. It was obviously a family portrait, a man, woman, and a young blonde headed girl with blue eyes. Hearing Mr. Marshall speaking, she turned her attention on her host.

"I guess you had the Ashton family to buy for, not to mention your big family." He waited for the butler to pass out the mugs of hot chocolate. "Thank you, Theodore, that will be all." William blew across the hot drink as the butler exited the room. "Who brought you to town to help you shop? Your grandmother?"

"No sir, I came into town with the Farrell sisters on their way to their café and bakery." Hattie slowly sipped her hot chocolate and some of the melting marshmallow stuck to her upper lip. William looked down and smiled to himself, as she continued to speak. "I did all the shopping all by myself William and got everything on my list, wrapped and promised to be delivered to my daddy at the market. I'll be going back with him when he closes the farm stand."

"Your grown-ups let you come to town shopping all alone?" he sat up, concern in his deep voice "If you were my daughter, I would see to it that you had a chaperon!"

"I'm very mature for ten-years-old Mr. Marshall." Hattie felt happy that her new friend cared about her welfare and it brought a question to her mind "Do you have children William? I noticed the painting over the mantle and the gentleman in the picture looks just like you."

"The gentleman in the painting bears a striking resemblance to me because he happens to be my great-great grandfather, William Franklin Marshall, the first." He stood up and went in front of the painting. Hattie got up and joined him, so she could see it closer.

"Then that is Susanne Marshall and their daughter, Pattie!" Hattie's eyes were glued on the beautiful little girl who smiled back at her. "Great-great Aunt Hattie's dearest friend!"

"You've heard about their close friendship?" Mr. Marshall

looked down at the young girl he had grown to love. "Did the stories come down from the past?"

"My parents and grandparents have told me many stories past down from one generation to the next, but most of my information came from Aunt Pattie, herself." Hattie felt his hand touch her shoulder and she looked up into his serious face. "Not her ghost William, her diary she left, just for me to read and solve the mystery for her."

"The mystery?" taking Hattie's hand, Mr. Marshall pulled her over on the sofa next to him "Are you referring to the mystery of their disappearance Hattie?"

"It was my Aunt Hattie's request that the next girl born to the Russel household, would be named Hattie, after her, and that she would get all her most precious possessions, which had been hidden in our attic ever since Aunt Hattie died in 1894, at ninety-years-old." Hattie reached for her mug and drank down the remainder of the hot chocolate before continuing "Among her things was her personal diary, a Christmas gift given to her in 1814 by her best friend, Pattie Marshall. My aunt had all their last moments together written down in that beautiful diary and it was packed with clues for me to go on."

"Hattie, are you some sort of young detective? Are you here to perhaps learn more clues to piece this mystery together?" his smile broke her tense feeling. "Perhaps, we can both share some of what we know and together we can solve this case once and for all."

Chapter 14

"Jumping Jupiter! That would be swell William! I mean, you've got the keys to the old mansion and I believe our answer lies inside that shut up old house!' Hattie found herself growing excited "There was a full moon on Christmas Eve in 1814 and the moon will be full again this Christmas Eve!"

"You really don't think there's still something inside that house, do you, my friend? It's been two-hundred-years since they vanished!"

"William, please don't think I'm being childish and I'm living in a fairy tale. I honestly believe there is something in that attic and it's evil!" Hattie notice a dark cloud fall over Mr. Marshall and she shuttered with a chill, even though the room was very warm. She thought it best to change the subject for the time being. "You never did tell me if you had any children, William?"

"I had a daughter, several years ago, but she died when she was ten, same age as you." William stood up and walked over to the painting again "She too had blonde hair and blue eyes, much like Pattie. It took me a long time to get over her loss."

"Is your wife gone too William?" her heart was breaking for her new friend and she wondered if that was why he took to her so. He stood, staring at the people in the painting. Hattie reached for his hand and he looked down "Did you lose your wife too?"

"It was an accident. They were killed instantly." His look was sad but tender "I just thanked God they didn't suffer."

"I'm truly sorry William. I shouldn't have brought it up. Please except my apology, my friend."

"Come now." Mr. Marshall noticed the genuine tears filling Hattie's brown eyes "Friends should be able to say what's on the mind and heart, right?"

Hattie took around him and gave him a loving hug "I'm glad we're friends, William, mystery or no mystery."

"But we do have a mystery to solve dear girl." He took her hand and led her back to the sofa "Let me start by telling you what I know." Hattie sit up, ears perked. "I was named after my Great-great grandfather, just like my grandfather and my own father, all who passed away in their early fifties. I guess I beat the odds or the spell has been broken." William took her hands in his "I have lived to see my 70th birthday."

"Seventy?" Hattie's eyes were big as saucers "You…look well for your age William." She swallowed.

"Good genes on my mother's side. She lived to be ninety-nine and looked remarkably young up until she was seventy." He winked at her "So I was given the name William Franklin Marshall the forth."

"Aunt Hattie did say she saw Mr. Marshall on Christmas night. She heard him call out Pattie's name and she turned around, hoping to see her friend Pattie but all she saw was the crying man walking quickly to her. Mr. Marshall must have thought he had seen his daughter because she had given Aunt Hattie her brand- new Christmas dress and he recognized the gift he had given her the evening before Christmas Eve." Hattie took a breath, knowing she had Mr. Marshall's full attention. "Aunt Hattie said he grabbed her weeping, saying he was glad she had got away from something he called, 'it'.

When Hattie ask him if Pattie was alright and told him that she was afraid for her, he looked up at her with wild eyes and accused her of stealing the dress. She assured him Pattie had brought it by on Christmas Eve and gave it to her, wrapped up, in a gold chest. Pattie ask her to wait and unwrap it on Christmas morning. Hattie said Mr. Marshall shook her unmercifully then ran to his carriage and drove out of town like a mad man." Hattie turned to face her friend "You said Mr. Marshall was your great-great grandfather, so did he get married to someone after leaving Sleepy Creek?"

"No friend, William Marshall never got married again, nor did he ever get over losing his family." William Marshall looked away, like he was thinking "The stories passed down to me say he began drinking heavily and often visited the town's tavern where, pardon my blunt talk, where prostitutes sold their wares."

"You mean, these wicked ladies sold their body to gentleman, like Mr. Marshall!" Hattie looked thoughtful "So, he slipped up and made this prostitute pregnant with your grandfather, William the second. I guess that meant he took responsibility for the baby and gave him his name."

"You are indeed wise Hattie Russel and your quick mind for deduction is amazing for someone so young." Mr. Marshall shook his head in admiration. "You are correct, Marshall raised the innocent bastard, knowing living with a prostitute for a mother was no place for a child. He paid her off and moved to Boston with a newborn baby."

"Then, the baby grew up, got married and became your grandfather, who had your father." Hattie was feeling real comfortable talking to her new friend and she admired him for treating her like an adult instead of a mere child. "How long has Mr. Johnson been your butler, William? He appears to be very protecting of you."

"Noticed that, did you?" Mr. Marshall laughed "Theodore has been with me for sixty years, ever since I turned ten, like yourself. Father wanted someone around to watch after me when he passed away. Like all the Marshall's before me, father knew his life would be cut short."

"That's real sad William, to fret over dying young. You know what I think, I think it helped put them in the ground, all that worrying "Hattie's mind went back to 1814 and Hattie's words "Pattie was real scared for her daddy, William, about his worrying about dying. She…" Hattie heard the clock on the mantle strike two-thirty and sit straight up "Golly gee, I've got to get going! Daddy packs up and leaves the square at three!"

"Then you mustn't be late child." Mr. Marshall picked up a small silver bell and rang it. "I'll get Mr. Johnson to walk with you back to the town square Hattie, so do not argue." He stood up and offered his hand. "Before you leave, I have a gift for you." Mr. Marshall walked over to a small closet and pulled out a big box wrapped in red paper, adorned with a large white bow. "Now this is an early Christmas gift. To a friend, from a friend. There is a dance at the club house on Friday night, December 23 and I would like to escort you there as my very special date." He smiled when her eyes lit up "Do you think I'm too old for such a pretty young lady?"

"Gosh no, William! I'd be proud to go with you to the dance, although I might be too short if we try to dance."

"Not if you're dancing on my feet or in my arms." Mr. Marshall walked her to the door where the butler was waiting "I'll be by to pick you up around seven. Does that agree with you Hattie?"

"It does William! School is out and I can stay up for the dance."
She held tight to the beautiful box "Maybe we can talk about the
mystery on our date. Christmas Eve will be the following day and I
just gotta go to your mansion that night!"

"We can discuss our mystery all you like my friend, but for now,
it's quarter till three and you've got a long track back to town."
William Marshall bent down and hugged her "Not to worry Hattie
Russel, your father knows you'll be there, he has your packages to
pack!"

"Yes, he does!" she gave him a big squeeze "Thank you for my
gift! I'm still working on yours! I know you will like it!"

"If you made it, I will cherish it Hattie." He motioned them
away, turned and went back inside the old stone house.

Chapter 15

"Hi daddy, did you get all my packages?" Hattie watched as her father and brother Andrew started to load the tailor with all her gifts. "Mickie's Hardware, the Marshall outlet store, Sleepy Creek toy shop and Libby's Bookstore, that's about it." Adam started handing Andrew the smaller packages and turned to smile at his daughter "You've been quite the busy shopper Hattie." He noticed the large gift she had clutched in her hands "Another gift? Won't me to store it on the wagon with all the others and you can take down our signs while we pack."

"Thanks daddy. Try not to set anything on it, it's pretty special." She watched him place her gift from Mr. Marshall in a safe spot then walked back to the signs. Hattie was busy taking down the farm sale sign and didn't noticed the pretty girl walking up next to her.

"Hello Hattie, I guess I got here too late to buy apples." Shannon Brower smiled "I wanted to thank you for saving my little brother Bart last evening from running into that big tree on the top slope."

"I only did what any good Christian girl would do Shannon, same as you did to save my brother Thomas by stopping Bradley from wreaking him." Hattie returned her beautiful smile as she continued stacking up the sale postures. She couldn't help but notice how Shannon kept looking in Andrew's direction. "Shannon, if you like my brother Andrew, go speak to him. He won't bite, honest."

"I'm not sure Andrew would not appreciate a Brower talking to him in a friendly way." The Brower girl's attention went back to Hattie "I'm sure he re-guards me as the enemy."

"Andrew is a warm caring man, Shannon. Just last night before the sled race, he told my brothers to be gentlemen and treat you like a lady."

"Did he?" Shannon watched as Andrew loaded up the new red bike and sighed "Is he going to the Christmas dance with anyone?"

"Let's go ask him." Hattie took her hand "Let me do the talking."

"I'm not sure Hattie." Shannon pulled back. "Maybe it will be better if I just left."

Joan Byrd

"And I say, if you like Andrew and he likes you, give it a shot!" Hattie thought this might be what was needed to stop the hate between the Russel's and the Brower's. She walked up to the wagon and called her brother's name. Turning, his eyes met Shannon's.

"Andrew, did you have any apples left? Shannon got here a few minutes after three and started to leave until I told her I'd check with you." Hattie gave him a knowing look "I'm sure you might be able to help a lady if there's any left."

"I would like nothing more than to help such a pretty lady." Andrew hopped down from the wagon and wiped off his hands "It appears we are all out of apples though." Shannon looked down, wondering if he really meant, no more for a Brower. Her heart fluttered when Andrew's fingers gently lifted her face "But not to worry, fair Shannon, we have loads of apples back on the farm and I will deliver as many as you need first thing Monday morning, right on your doorstep."

"Aren't you afraid to come to my house Andrew? I know my brothers can be real mean to you Russel men." She looked embarrassed "I truly wish all the bickering and fighting would just stop but there's been a feud going on between our families for generations."

"I never let a bully keep me from doing my job." Andrew's smile was warm and real "If a customer orders our produce during the week, it's our policy to deliver. Grant, you, it's always either daddy or grandpa this time of year, who makes the delivery. Mama needs all her boys at the factory the week before Christmas." Andrew took her hand "This is one delivery I wish to make, if you promise to be the one to answer the door."

"That is terribly sweet Andrew, but if your mama needs you..." Shannon was cut off.

"I can bring it by on my way to the cookie factory, and I won't take no Shannon Brower." There was something about this pretty girl that made Andrew's heart race. "It's the least I can do after you save my little brother's butt on the slopes last night."

"It's time someone in my family show a little respect and kindness to others, especially..." she looked up shyly, making her that much more alluring to the young twenty-year-old. "especially you...Russel's

"Shannon, have you been asked to the Christmas dance next

76

Friday night?" Andrew suddenly felt it was time to show his feelings for Shannon and he was sure she had feeling for him as well.

"I have been asked…" Shannon noticed Andrew's sudden sad expression, so she reached up and touched his handsome face "like I was saying, two boys have asked me to go, but I told them I was expecting someone else to invite me and he has! Yes, Andrew, I would love to go to the dance with you!"

"That's…'wonderful'!" Andrew almost laughed with joy "I will pick you up at seven, if that is alright with you?"

"Friday night, seven o'clock! I'll be ready!' Shannon smiled brightly and started to leave when she twirled back around "Oh, and I will be waiting by the front door Monday morning for my order, Mr. Russel!" she turned away, smiling and looked up toward heaven and whispered, "Thank you God!"

"You heard correctly, I said, I 'm taking Shannon Brower to the Christmas dance!" Andrew looked around at all the shocked faces "It's high time someone handed out an olive branch!"

"Son, do you expect the Brower's will allow their daughter to date you?" Adam had mixed feelings over the situation. On one hand, he was proud of his eldest son trying to bring peace between two long rivals, but had the distrust and hate between the Russel's and the Brower's gone on too long to change. "This family hates the sight of any Russel, Andrew. You might get hurt if you go through with this."

"I'll take my chances, daddy." Andrew looked at the one family member he knew understood, Hattie. "I think when someone has feelings for another and they feel the exact way about you, then you just follow your heart, right Hattie?"

"Yes, I do Andrew." Hattie stood up and walked over to him. Taking his hand, she turned toward the big family. "I've seen the love written on Shannon and Andrew ever since the season games and I agree with Andrew, this new love between enemies can bind us all together in Christian love!"

Andrew squeezed her in his arms "Unlike the Hatfield's and the McCoy's, we can find common ground and make peace with one another."

"As long as it does not end up like Romeo and Juliet!" Carolyn laid down her book and looked up serious "Andrew, your heart's in the right place son, but to be on the safe side, Monday morning I insist you take Peter and Phillip with you when you deliver those apples. You might have a lot of unhappy brothers waiting to throw your apples back at you."

"Your mother is right about the delivery on Monday, but son, you'll be on your own Saturday night when you pick up Shannon." Adam Russel looked concerned "You could get yourself in trouble going alone at night."

"Look, daddy, I refuse to have one of my brothers tagging along on my date with Shannon." Andrew felt like his special night with the girl he was crazy about was about to be ruined, until he was saved by his little sister.

"Andrew and Shannon can come with me and my date!" every single Russel turned to stare at Hattie.

"Your date? Good heavens child, what are you talking about?" Nettie had been knitting the last sweater for Drake Ashton and listened with interest up until her granddaughter announce she had a date for the dance.

"Hattie, if you tell us Bart Brower ask you and his daddy is taking you both, I think I will throw up!" Matthew blurted out.

"No Matthew! I would just as soon date a frog than that ungrateful bully!" Hattie frowned at her brother "My date is grown-up, extremely mature, and very handsome for a man, seventy -years-old!"

"Baby girl, you know I'd like nothing more than to take you to that Christmas dance, but my Nettie might get jealous." Gideon thought she was referring to him, knowing he would do almost anything for Hattie.

Hattie giggled at the thought "Grandpa, it would be real swell if you took your lovely wife to that dance, and daddy ask mama, but my date ask me today when I was in town. He said he would come by and pick me up around seven, so Andrew can inform Shannon it will be a little after seven."

"Hattie, I know we all are anxious to find out who ask you." Andrew lifted her chin up "Who is this 'older' man in your life?"

"William was gracious enough to ask me and I excepted! He even gave me a gift, the big red box with the white bow. He asked me to unwrap it and use it Friday night. It has to be my very own evening gown."

The Box in the Attic

The room was filled with stunned silence until Carolyn Russel stood up and walked next to her smiling daughter.

"William Franklin Marshall is coming out here, to the farm, and pick you up as…his date?"

"Yes mama! William and I are very good friends and I'm sure he would be happy to give Andrew and Shannon a ride to the country club." Hattie smiled up at her brother "We could even be chaperons for the two love birds if it would make all of you feel better."

"I think I'm the one that needs to chaperon you and William, little sister." Andrew couldn't resist a chuckle "Boy, speaking of winter and spring relationships."

"Andrew, get real! William and I do love one another, but not in a mushy way!" Hattie laughed along with her brother at the ideal of them being romantic. "We are close friends who are both interested in the same mystery. With his help, the mystery of the Marshall's disappearance can be solved."

"And I suppose you plan to go with your new friend to that old mansion and look around." Nettie joined those standing, growing anxious over the real reason this strange man had suddenly took an interest in her granddaughter. Her eyes fell on Gideon whose attention was focused on Hattie. "Gideon Russel, maybe taking me to that Christmas dance isn't such a bad ideal. I do enjoy a good slow dance with you, old man."

"Now Nettie, we might be interfering with these kids plans." Gideon winked at Andrew "I wouldn't want them to think we were there just to spy on their fun."

"Nonsense old man, spy? The very idea!" Nettie patted Carolyn's back "Why don't you and Adam join us. I think a night out will do us all a world of good."

"What about you other boys? Do you want to ask a girl to the dance? I'm sure Hattie's date, Mr. Marshall can get tickets for everyone, since he owns the Marshall Country Club." Carolyn laughed softly at her son's faces, then put her arm around her daughter. "Do you think your friend could come up with sixteen more tickets, unless Andrew hasn't got his two yet?"

"My two tickets are tucked safely away mama." Andrew narrowed his eyes, upset with the turn of events. Hattie could tell he was upset so she thought of a good solution she would share with him when they were alone.

"Mama, I'm sure William can come up with sixteen tickets, if you're serious about going."

"I'm quite serious Hattie!" Carolyn turned to her husband "Brush up on your dance steps sweetheart! You're taking me to the Christmas dance."

"I wouldn't miss the chance to hold you in my arms again on the dance floor, Carolyn Russel." Adam reached over to Peter "Got your eye on a girl son? How 'bout the rest of you boys?"

"Not me! I will be perfectly happy staying right here Friday night!" Matthew grunted "There's not a girl in Sleepy Creek I fancy!"

"Me either! I'll stay home with Matthew and watch the football game." Thomas threw his feet on the footstool!"

Peter, Philip, James, and John all had someone in mind, so the ticket count dropped to twelve. Andrew grew quiet and excused himself. Hattie slipped away to catch him while the others discussed what they would be wearing.

Hattie caught him at the top of the stairs. "Cheer up Andrew, the country club is a big place and I'll ask William to place the family at the other end of the big room so you and Shannon can have your privacy."

"Hattie Russel, you are a living doll! If you were not my little sister, I'd ask you to the dance myself!" Andrew laughed as he hugged her and danced off to his bedroom.

Chapter 16

"Thanks grandma for bringing me with you shopping." Hattie looked around at the crowded streets, bustling with shoppers. "It will give me a chance to go visit my friend and ask him about the dance tickets."

"And maybe a wee bit of investigating the Marshall mystery while you're there?" Nettie held her granddaughter's hand tightly, not wanting to lose her in the hustle and bustle. "Did you call Mr. Marshall like I ask? It is a busy time for him too and he may have meetings this morning."

"I called him early this morning, and after chatting to Mr. Johnson, his butler, William came on the line." Hattie waved at the Farrell sisters through the Bakery window as they passed by, then continued "William said he could see me this morning, but his afternoon was tied up with business." She stopped outside the lady's dress shop, Margaret's Fashion, where Nettie was going to buy a new gown for the dance. "Grandma, it might take you awhile in there and I wouldn't want to hold William up. His cottage is just down the street from here."

"Yes, I can see it just down that small hill." Nettie turned her granddaughter around to face her "Hattie, you may go now, but you must not hold the man up chatting about that mystery. Just ask him about the tickets and come straight back here. I will be waiting for you."

"I'll try to make my visit brief grandma, unless, William ask about the mystery." Hattie gave her a sweet smile "Take your time shopping and don't just grab the first dress you like. Try on several. It's not every day Nettie Russel gets to buy an evening gown!" she winked and hurried off down the sidewalk.

"Oh, it's you." Theodore Johnson lifted his eyebrow as he stared down at the smiling ten-year-old "Mr. Marshall did say he was expecting you. Do come in young lady and wait out here in the hall while I inform Mr. Marshall of your arrival." He turned slowly and made his way up the stairs. Hattie looked around at the elegant entry hall with its fine paintings. Taking a closer look at a woman with child, she smiled to herself.

"Mrs. Fisher, my friend William is quite religious." Remembering the book store owner's comments about Mr. Marshall being a heathen "Such a lovely painting of the Virgin Mary and Baby Jesus! It's looks so real!" her eyes fell on the artist "Rembrandt? I think that's what it's sign, the signature is so faded."

"Admiring the gentleman's art work?" the butler walked up next to Hattie "Mr. Marshall does have an eye for art and he prefers the masters."

"The masters? Is Mr. Masters better than this painter?" Hattie had never seen the old master painters work before and was confused as to how anything else could be better than this beautiful work of art. "If William ever wants to replace this one with one of Mr. Masters, tell him I would love to have it."

"I just bet you would, Hattie Russel but Mr. Marshall won't be parting with his paintings ever!" Mr. Johnson cleared his throat. "Now, if you will be so good as to follow me." He led her to the sitting room with the stone fireplace where the Marshall family's portrait was hanging. "Wait here in the parlor, Miss Russel. Mr. Marshall will be down shortly." He started to walk away, then turned to face the young girl "And do not touch anything, please!" with that, he walked from the sitting room.

Hattie walked over to the mantle to look at the painting and she felt a chill run down her back, even though there was a warm fire burning in the hearth. She focused in on the pretty girl smiling back.

"Pattie, I promised my aunt, your best friend Hattie, that I would find you." Hattie looked around to be sure she was still alone, she didn't feel good being alone with Mr. Johnson. There was something about him she did not trust. "I know it's been two hundred years since you vanished, but come Christmas Eve, I will know the truth!"

"I just bet you will, my friend." Hearing the familiar voice, Hattie turned to a smiling Mr. Marshall "I trust Theodore wasn't too demanding of you Hattie, he can be a bit bossy at times."

"I can take care of myself, William, besides, I've been around pushy people before and I simply listen to them giving orders and politely nod my head." Hattie smiled when her friend chuckled at her "As for solving the mystery, I shall not rest on Christmas Eve until I find out what happen."

"Then I will help you the best I can, little darling." William motioned to the sofa and joined her "I really must leave in about thirty minutes though, so we will have to wait to discuss our mystery another time."

"I understand, truly. Besides, my grandma is expecting me to return to Margaret's Fashion Store soon."

"You mentioned something on the telephone about tickets to the Christmas dance." He picked up a pipe and filled it with good smelling tobacco. "Has someone ask you to get them some?"

"You could say that." Hattie turned to face him and took a breath of the smoke coming from his pipe "Mumm, that's real nice, the smell from your pipe!" Mr. Marshall just smiled, so she continued "Let me go back a little. My oldest brother Andrew ask Shannon Brower to go with him to the Christmas dance Friday night."

"Are the Brower's the ones who cheated at the season games?' Hattie nodded yes "And aren't they the ones your family has been in a feud with for generations?"

"Yes sir, the very same. That's why my family were alarmed at Andrew's announcement. They were making a terrible fuss over it so I intervened and told them that Andrew and Shannon could ride with me and my date. They didn't like the ideal of Andrew going to pick her up at the Brower's in the dark."

"Hattie, how did they take you going on a date?" William Marshall sat up, wanting to hear what her family had to say about him asking their little girl to a grown- up dance.

"At first, everyone was speechless, then my grandmother spoke up and wanted to know what I was talking about. I think she thought the idea was preposterous, me, going on a date. Then Matthew, my fifteen-year-old brother asked me if it was stupid Bart Brower and I told him I would rather date a frog than that ungrateful bully!"

"Good for you!" William remembered how the Brower brat treated Hattie at the games. "How did your parents take the truth, that you were dating me, a man of seventy?"

"Shocked. At least at first but after a while they started getting creative. First it was my grandma Nettie. I think I might have put the ideal in her head when I told them I was dating a mature, handsome man

Who was seventy." Hattie laughed remembering her grandpa's statement. "Grandpa Gideon thought I was referring to him and said he would love to take me, but it might make his Nettie jealous. I told him that was a swell ideal, to take grandma. So suddenly, she felt like dancing."

"So, your grandparents want to come to keep an eye on you and Andrew." He smiled "You need tickets for them?"

"And Mama, daddy, Peter, Philip, James, John, and their dates, so that makes twelve tickets total." Hattie sat back and took a breath "Andrew was upset about the family's obvious spy game, so I told him I'd ask you to see that they were seated at the far end of the big ball room and Andrew and Shannon at the other end." Hattie looked up pleadingly "Do you think you could do this…for me, please?"

"You are quite the charmer, Hattie Russel." The butler stuck his head inside the door and pointed at his watch "Your tea is ready sir and you only have fifteen minutes before I take you to your meeting."

"Very well Theodore, bring in the tea." He looked down at Hattie "Would you care for something?"

"Not for me sir, I must be leaving soon." Hattie liked her new friend very much "Grandma said I shouldn't hold you up William."

"Very smart grandmother you have child." Theodore mumbled "I shall get your tea sir and have a spot of tea myself before departing.

"That's fine, Johnson. Just watch that British talk" William frowned at the butler "The accent does not suit you. Go man, I'll see my guest out." He stood up and offered his hand.

"Theodore use to do broad way and he relished getting to play a Brit." Mr. Marshall helped Hattie with her coat "As for the tickets, tell your family I would be more than happy to get them twelve last minute tickets although I cannot guarantee where they will be seated." He winked "Just between you and me, I know exactly where I will have them sitting and I promise you, my lovely date, they will be nowhere close to Andrew and his date or you and your date." Taking her hand, William Marshall walked Hattie to the door.

"You and I will have the best table in the great hall, my beautiful young date." Mr. Marshall bent down and hugged her "Your brother and his date are welcome to join us my dear in the car going over to the country club." He patted the top of her head "And this painting you admired so much, will be yours one day. A gift to a friend, from a friend."

"Racing sea horses! William, you're the best friend ever!" Hattie felt tears coming in her eyes as she hugged him tightly "I love you for you William and it wouldn't matter if you ever gave me anything, as long as I have you!"

Feeling tears himself, Mr. Marshall returned her hug.

"I feel the same way about you Hattie." He opened the door back "Be careful walking back up the hill my friend and I'll see you Friday night."

"I'll be ready William." She wrapped the scarf tighter to ward off the cold wind "Enjoy your tea!" with that, Hattie walked happily up the hill as William Franklin Marshall watched her until she was out of sight.

Chapter 17

The week was flying by for Hattie as her work load on the farm got busier. Now she did not only have the girl's chores in the house, like cleaning, dishes, and laundry but her outside chores had picked up from gathering hen eggs to, feeding the chickens and hogs, not to mention their old collie, Jack.

Tuesday morning brought yet another snow to Sleepy Creek, but that wouldn't stop the Russel's plans to deliver the Ashton's Christmas tree and all their gifts Hattie had purchased. The Russell boys had loaded up the big smaller wagon with the tree and gifts, along with all the decorations and Christmas lights from the U.M.Y.F. from church. As many of the youth that could come and help decorate the tree promised to be there around seven p.m.

The plan was that while the youth kept the three Ashton children busy with the big tree, Hattie, Andrew, and Philip would meet Drake Ashton in their garage for the gifts from Santa. To their relief, all their plans went well, when at last Hattie and her two older brothers brought in the rest of the presents to place under the twinkling tree.

"Wow! Sparkling, sugar candy canes! What a magnificent Christmas tree!" she laid a big box under its branches, as the three Ashton children raced over and knelt down to watch as she took the presents from her brothers to place around the tree. "Kids, I think this is about the prettiest Christmas tree in Sleepy Creek!"

"I agree little sister, all of you have done a wonderful job with the decorations." Andrew's eyes fell on Shannon Brower "I'm glad you decided to go to the Christmas workshop Shannon. I see a lot of new decorations, all hand made." He walked over with the last gifts and looked over the tree. He noticed one ornament in particular, a girl and boy skating together. Andrew's eyes lit up as he looked down at the girl he loved. "You made this one."

"I did Andrew." Shannon looked down shyly "It's a couple skating together." As he reached for her hand, she smiled "I was thinking about our date Friday night and I made two young lovers dancing on skates."

"How mushy is that!" Matthew chuckled

"Give it a rest, little brother!" Andrew hit his arm "You're just jealous because you don't have a date for the dance."

"Jealous?" Matthew laughed "I could have asked any one of these girls…" he whispered, "but I want a real woman, just like…" Matthew rubbed Hattie's head "just like my baby sister's male date, mature and experienced in love."

"Now that is funny Matthew!" Andrew hit his arm a little harder as he frowned down at his outspoken brother "You know perfectly well that Mr. Marshall and Hattie are just good friends. Besides, they got the Marshall mystery in common, so that makes them closer."

"Matthew knows all that Andrew, he just likes to be cute." Hattie stood up and smiled at Shannon Brower. "Thank you for helping the church youth on their Christmas project this year. I'm sure they were glad to have your help, you're very talented in art." Hattie's mind went to William's painting of the Virgin Mary and Baby Jesus. It was the prettiest work of art she had ever seen, so absentmindedly she spoke out. "I think my very favorite artist is a man named Rembrandt, I think that's his name. It wasn't clear on William's painting of Mary and Jesus."

"Your friend William Marshall has a painting of Rembrandt? One of the old master painters of all time!" Shannon could not believe her ears. "I've seen copies of the Virgin Mary and Baby Jesus and they were way over my budget. The original is priceless! I knew Mr. Marshall was rich, but to own such a painting as that! I wonder what other paintings he has?"

"William has loads of pretty paintings, Shannon." Hattie was thoughtful as she could still see her dear friend standing at the mantle, staring at the family portrait of the 1814 Marshall's. "Of all the paintings my friend possesses, the painting over the mantle is his favorite. The first William Marshall, his wife Susanne and their daughter Pattie."

"So now you know what they look like kid-o." Andrew hugged his sister "Does William Franklin Marshall, your friend, look anything like his relative?"

"William is the perfect image of his great-great-grandfather, William Marshall, the first!" Hattie knew she had everyone's attention "That makes my friend, William the forth and I'm sad to say, the last. His only child was a girl and she, along with William's wife, were killed in a terrible accident."

"What sort of accident?" Matthew had walked over to hear more about this man no one knew nothing about, and suddenly he was pouring his heart out to their little sister. "How old was his daughter when she died?"

"She was my age, if you must know, and I can read your mind Matthew, and the answer is, no, that is not why William has taken a liken to me! It's much deeper and I don't expect you to understand because you find it hard to be serious." Hattie walked over and put on her coat "As for how the mother and daughter died, I haven't the slightest idea Matthew, I let my friend tell me just what he wants me to know." Her gaze fell on Andrew.

"Andrew, I think we need to go so the Ashton's can enjoy their beautiful Christmas tree together."

"Of course, you're right Hattie." Still holding to Shannon's hand, the oldest Russel boy led the way outside "Shannon, can we give you a lift home?"

"That's very sweet Andrew and I would like nothing more if it wasn't for my daddy's car waiting in the church parking lot." Shannon smiled and squeezed Andrew's hand "I road in the church van with Mr. Patterson and the other youth. See you Friday?"

"I'll be there in style!" Andrew smiled "Hattie's date will be giving us a lift in his car, so it will be closer to 7:15, just be ready, pretty girl." One last hand embrace, and the couple pulled apart and went their separate ways.

The night of the big Christmas dance had come and Hattie had opened her gift from Mr. Marshall, the prettiest gown she had ever laid her eyes on. She imagined herself as a princess when she looked into her floor length mirror on her bathroom door. Then her attention went to her hair and she saw just plain Hattie Russel looking back.

"Golly gee Millie, I look like a country bunking trying to look all grown up!" Hattie picked up her hair brush to see what she could do different to improve her simple hairstyle. "Darn Millie, it's no use! How could I ever look good enough for my dashing handsome date! William will see me as a child, a little girl!"

"You are a little girl Hattie." Carolyn had come to help her daughter with her hair, so it would match the lovely evening gown Mr. Marshall had given her. "You cannot change that fact dear, but

I can help you fix you pretty hair to match your gown." She had her to sit down as she took her brush and began brushing her hair up.

"Thank you, mama. I just want to look extra pretty tonight for William. He was nice enough to ask me instead of one of the single women in town." Hattie watched as her mother worked wonders with her dark brown hair. "You don't suppose I could put on a little blush on my cheeks and lipstick to match the dress?"

"Are you trying to look older young lady?" Carolyn smiled as she pulled her blush and light rose lipstick from her pocket. "I'll help you put these on when I have finished with your hair."

"Mama. You're the best!" Hattie beamed "We ladies have to look beautiful for our dates, right?"

"You are correct, my dear. Especially you Hattie. It's not every day William Franklin Marshall ask a lady out on a date!' Carolyn stood back to check out her masterpiece. She had swept up the dark locks into a bund with loose ringlets hanging down the back and around her face. Hattie stared at the girl in the mirror as her mother applied light make-up on her, then stood back, smiling. "Hattie Russel, you will melt every man's heart tonight at that dance."

"I only wish to melt one man's heart mama, and now…" Hattie stood up to find a princess looking back "and now William can be proud of his date!"

"You've grown very fond of Mr. Marshall, haven't you sweetheart?" Carolyn felt in her pocket for the two small boxes and smiled.

"I can't explain my feeling for William mama, I just know they're real." Hattie grew serious "I love William very much and he loves me, he said so."

"Hattie, it's good to have that very special someone in your life you can call a true friend." Carolyn had mixed feelings over her daughter's statement. It was as though her little girl was growing up overnight, and far too soon. "You said Mr. Marshall's daughter was ten when she died, maybe he has replaced her in his heart for you." Carolyn noticed Hattie's sad expression "Hattie dear, does it matter why he loves you? Is not his love for you all that matters?"

"His love for me is all that matters mama." Hattie looked down, fighting the tears she felt coming "I couldn't bare life without William in it. He is the same age as grandpa, but William looks like he's much younger. Because he's older than I am, he'll probably die sooner than me, then I would feel like Aunt Hattie and never get over my loss."

"Hattie, we cannot think of death as a separation from those we love. We can't change life, no matter how hard we would like to." Carolyn reached for her daughter and hugged her "It would hurt me terribly bad if your grandparents or your daddy went before me, and God forbid that any of my beautiful nine children go first, but child, we cannot change the will of our Lord. You must put your faith in the lord, Hattie, and just enjoy what time you have with your William."

"Thank you, mama, for everything." Hattie forced a smile "I guess I better put on my cheerful face, for you and William."

"That a girl! Now I got you two early Christmas gifts, so you can wear them tonight." Carolyn pulled out the two boxes and handed them to her daughter. One was a good smelling perfume and the other was a strand of pearls, a gift previously given to Carolyn Russel on her wedding day from her mother.

"Oh, mama, your pearls! I don't know what to say, they mean so much to you." Hattie held out the white strand of pearls carefully for her mother to place around her slim neck.

"I was going to save them and give the to you on your wedding day, but I knew how important this night was to my baby girl." Carolyn now was the one to fight tears as she fastened the beautiful keepsake on her daughter. "Now hurry and spray on some perfume, not a lot, it pretty strong" she reached down and kissed Hattie's cheek. "Now I'm off to get in my gown so my date will be happy to escort his date to the dance."

"You are a beautiful couple mama. I just hope I look half as good as you when I grow up." Hattie watched her mother smile, then walk quickly to their room. Seven would be here soon and so would Hattie's date, William Marshall.

Chapter 18

Matthew and Thomas sat at the living room window looking out for William Marshall's car, each brother trying to guess which expensive kind would be driving in. They both sat up, noses against the cold glass when they heard what sounded like horse hooves coming on the dirt road. Then they saw the big carriage with a driver decked out in a top hat, coming up to the house.

"Ah shit! A horse and carriage!" Matthew whispered to his brother "Our little sister will think she really is Cinderella tonight!"

"Boys, move away from that window before Mr. Marshall sees you spying!" Adam Russel came down the steps in his new suit. "Didn't I here Marshall drive up?"

Matthew sat back, smiling at his handsome father "Looking good daddy-o!" he walked over to the front door "You heard Mr. Marshall alright, coming in his carriage! I'll get the door."

"Step aside Matthew and try to act grown up!" Adam pulled at his tie and opened the door when the bell rang. William Marshall waited on the other side, dressed in a handsome long black wool coat covering what appeared to be a black silk tuxedo. "Mr. Marshall, please come in. My daughter will be down shortly."

"Thank you, Mr. Russel. You have a lovely farm here and the good help to run it." He grew quiet when he noticed the beautiful young lady walking down the steps with a smile as lovely as her dress. "Hattie! How grown up you look tonight. Never have I seen a more radiant angel!"

"Yeh, all grown up for a little midget!" Matthew chuckled.

"I see you're still in your jeans young man, no date?" William Marshall frowned at the joking brother "But then I guess you are not ready to date girls, unlike your lovely sister. She will be the bell of the ball tonight and I know I shall have to keep the wolves at bay, so they won't sweep her out of my arms." He walked over and placed a beautiful cape around her shoulders, another gift he had brought her for this night.

"Are you ready to dance the night away with me, fair Hattie?"

"I am William, as long as I am dancing with my dashing date."

Kissing her daddy goodbye, Hattie took Williams arm and called up the stairs "Andrew, your ride is here!"

"Coming, sis!" Andrew came down looking sharp and ready for a romantic night with his girl "Let's go, fair Shannon is waiting."

"I like your choice of words Andrew." William led the way to the carriage and help Hattie up "There's blankets in the back seat my friend, just in case those love sparks are not enough to ward off the cold night air."

"A warm blanket and my arms will be all my girl will need Mr. Marshall." Andrew climbed to the rear of the big wagon as William took a seat beside Hattie. He turned around to the young man "You may call me William, Andrew, if we are to be family."

"A...yes sir, I mean William." Andrew sat back, wondering what the rich man was referring to.

"Are you warm enough sweetheart, under the wool blanket?" William put his arm around her shoulders and pulled her close "I'll help keep you warm."

"Thanks William." Hattie's eyes twinkled with happiness "This is where I belong, safe in your arms."

Mr. Marshall smiled and patted the driver on the back "To the Brower house Edwards, then to the country club." With just a soft 'very good, sir' the driver picked up his reigns and drove the carriage away.

The country club was ablaze with Christmas lights when the carriage pulled up to the steps where a footman was waiting to assist Mr. Marshall and his guest down from the high carriage. The footman, dressed in an outfit that dated back to the 1800's, opened the massive double doors for the owner of The Marshall Country Club, and bowed his head in respect. Another footman, in the same outfit, walked them to the table and pulled out the seats for Hattie and Shannon, then spoke privately with the owner and walked away.

The large ballroom was already buzzing with many well-dressed ticket holders and all their attention seem to be on Marshall's table and his guest. He bent down to whisper in Hattie's ear.

"I took the liberty to order our drinks little darling and as soon as they're served, I'll separate our privacy with your brother and his date." He smiled as she looked around, trying to figure out what he was talking about. "Not to worry Hattie darling, You, shall find out soon enough. Did I not tell you we would have the best seats in the ballroom?"

"You did William." She laughed softly "My brother seems to be happy with these arrangements, so you don't need to move him if it's a lot of bother."

"I won't be moving him pretty girl." He winked at her when the waiter set the drinks down and passed them around. After thanking him, William reached under the table and mashed a hidden button and a blush velvet curtain fell down around them, leaving a small opening, where they could see out, but the crowd of people could not see them. "The privacy I promise, my beautiful young date. They may see us when we dance, but we can have our privacy to talk together without a lot of gossiping women and rude whispers."

"This is real neat William, just the two of us in our own world." She picked up her drink and took a sip of her red drink "Mum, this is very sweet and good dear friend, what's it called?"

"Sherry, my dear, just like the young drink in Paris and Italy." William picked up his expensive wine and took a sip, letting his eyes fall on Hattie's young developing breast. "You are quite the young lady tonight, Miss Russel. You are budding into a very beautiful girl."

"Thank you, William. You are exceptionally handsome tonight yourself." Hattie took a small sip "I really loved the carriage ride. It was a pleasant surprise, William."

"I thought you might like it Hattie." His hand touched her face lovingly "It belonged to my great-great-grandfather William." His eyes held hers "You are very beautiful, my Hattie. Oh, to be young again."

"William, are you saying, if you were younger and I were a little older, we could become more than friends?" Hattie felt like she was dreaming and William had just confessed his love to her.

"Hattie Russel, why do you have to be so charming and mature acting? It merely makes me desire you more." He smiled and stood up, then offered his hand "May I have this dance Miss Russel? They're playing one of my favorite, 'For I Only Have Eyes, For You'!"

"I'd love to dance with you William." Hattie took his hand and walked out to the dance floor. Climbing on his boots, Hattie reached up to take his hand and he began waltzing her around the room as he sang the words to her.

"Are the stars out tonight? I don't know if it's cloudy or bright, for I only have eyes for you, dear…" slowly William Marshall pulled her up in his arms and continued singing in her ear as she hugged his neck tightly.

They danced the next three songs, then went back to their table, were a large plate of fruit and cheese had been placed and two fresh glasses of sherry and wine. Mr. Marshall helped his young date with her chair.

"I feel like a grown up tonight William and you make everything so special." Hattie reached for some cheese and took a bite, then a small sip of the sherry "Mumm, the cheese and sherry taste good together, like milk and cookies."

"Milk and cookies." William laughed softly "There's still a little girl in there, my little darling." He watched her closely as she enjoyed the cheese and fruit and let his mind wonder. "Hattie, how would you like to have dinner with me tomorrow evening at my cottage?"

Hattie looked up, her mouth full of cheese. Holding up her finger, signaling one second, she drank some water, then took a deep breath.

"Dinner? You mean supper?"

"Yes sweetheart, I mean supper." He smiled and touched her hand. "It gets lonely having to eat alone all the time, especially on the holidays."

"William, I'd love to have sup…dinner with you tomorrow evening, but I really need to ask my mama and daddy first." She looked down at his strong hand resting on hers. "We always attend the Christmas Eve services at church at seven p.m."

"Tell your parents we can have our dinner early, then I will escort you to the church services and afterward, we could go up to the mansion and solve the mystery." Seeing her bright smile, William knew he had won her heart "What do you say partner, dinner, service, then a trip to the old mansion on the hill, just you and me?"

"Golly gee, William, I've just gotta convince mama and daddy to let me come!" Hattie sat up, filled with excitement about going to the old house with William on Christmas Eve night.

"I know my girl can convince her parents when she sets her mind to it." Feeling better, William stood up and took her hand "May I have this dance with the prettiest girl here tonight?"

"Who, my mama?" Hattie teased.

"Funny too!" William helped her up "Your mother is a very pretty woman Hattie, but my heart belongs to her daughter."

Hattie had a real strange feeling in her stomach after hearing William's words and when he lifted her up into his arms to dance, she suddenly wished she was older, as her butterflies continued to flutter inside her stomach.

Feeling a little light headed from the dancing and the two glasses of sherry, Hattie let her date lift her up in the carriage. She could hear William talking to her parents and Andrew, but she couldn't make out his words. After a few minutes, he climbed up next to Hattie and wrapped the blanket and his arms around her trembling shoulders.

"My girl cold?" He slapped the driver's back and told him to drive slowly to the Russel farm, then turned his attention back on Hattie "Are you getting warm, sweet girl?"

"I think so, William." Hattie laid her spinning head on his shoulder "William, you forgot to ask your driver to take Shannon home first." She started to raise her head, but William held it close to his chest.

"Just stay put pretty girl and rest your head." William closed his eyes, knowing his true feeling for this mere child was ridicules, and yet he could not help the deep love he felt for her. In his mind, William Marshall couldn't explain why he had fallen in love with a ten-year-old girl, but his heart knew if she had been just eight years older, he would ask her to marry him.

"William, what about Shannon? She and Andrew are very quiet back there." Hattie managed to look up into his dark eyes.

"That's because they are not riding in the carriage Hattie." Mr. Marshall rubbed his fingers over her face "They road back with Mr. Johnson, in my car."

"But why William? You're already taking me home. Wouldn't it be out of Mr. Johnson's way to go to the same place?" Hattie sat up when her friend pulled out a thermos bottle and two mugs containing marshmallows. He poured the steaming hot chocolate over the fluffy marshmallows and handed her the warm cup.

Joan Byrd

"That should make you feel better darling." He blew across his cup as he talked "I got Theodore to take them home because I wanted to be alone with my best girl. It has been such a lovely night. I shall hate to say goodnight at the door."

"I had loads of fun tonight too, William." She took a careful sip of the hot chocolate and it warmed her all over. "You'll right, I'm beginning to feel much better, William."

"I'm glad." He watched her closely as he spoke "Hattie, can I ask you to keep a big secret for me?"

Hattie looked up innocently, admiring his handsome face in the moonlight. "Sure William, I will keep your secret. What is it?"

"This drink you had tonight, sherry, I would like you to keep it our secret Hattie. You must not tell anyone I gave it to you, Promise." She could tell her friend was very serious.

"Why William, will it get you in some kind of trouble?" William loved her innocents and mature understanding.

"If you told anyone Hattie, your parents would forbid you to see me again and I could even go to jail." His gazed held hers as she tried to sort out why drinking the sweet drink could keep her from William.

"William, what is it about this Sherry that makes it so dangerous to our relationship?" Hattie's words referring to them having a relationship made his heart race with desire. "Is that what made me start giggling before we left and feeling light headed when we were walking out to the carriage?"

"Hattie, remember when I told you young people in France and Italy drink sherry, the fact is they do over in Europe. They drink wine over there instead of water, or so I've read." He watched her eyes grow big as she sat straight up.

"Wine? Sherry is wine?" she collected her thoughts, suddenly realizing the hot chocolate was to take away her dizziness. "Jeepers! I had my first wine ever!" Hattie noticed William's concerned look and reached up and touched his face "Relax William, your secret is safe with me. I wouldn't let anything keep me away from you. I love you William Marshall!"

Mr. Marshall relaxed and pulled Hattie in his arms "I love you Hattie Russel. With all my heart!"

As they were approaching the farm house, Hattie suddenly remembered her date talking to her parents at the country club. She looked up and found him looking at the end of their journey, sadness on his face. Not wanting to upset him, Hattie chose her words carefully.

"William, what were you and my parents talking bout at the club house before you got on the carriage?"

"We were talking about a certain beautiful girl. My beautiful girl, Hattie." Mr. Marshall held her tight, dreading letting her go from his arms "I thought it best if I ask them about you having dinner with me tomorrow evening."

"Did you?" she sat up, excited "Did they say yes?"

"After I told them we would have an early dinner, so we could make the Christmas Eve services at church, they could find no reason to say no, dear one." His heart melted from her happy smile "I did ask them about me taking you to the mansion tomorrow night and they said they would have to think about that one and let me know."

"Oh, William, there's just gotta be a way to convince them!" Hattie grew anxious, being so close to solving the two-hundred-year old mystery, and the only thing standing in their way, was Adam and Carolyn Russel. "I'll think of something William!"

"I'm counting on you sweetheart." Knowing the carriage would be pulling up in the porch light soon, William bent over and took her pretty young face in his hands, then parted his lips over hers in the first real kiss Hattie had ever had. When he finally broke away, he smiled down at her dreamy expression, her eyes closed and a warm smile over her perfect lips. William gently touched her face and she opened her eyes, where they stared at one another in silence, letting the love they shared, speak In stillness.

Lifting her gently in his arms, he let her slide toward the ground, until her shoes touched the road. William and Hattie walked hand in hand up on the porch as Adam Russel open the door to collect his daughter. She smiled up at the man she cared so much about, not wanting to release his hand.

"Thank you, William, for everything! I shall never forget this night ever!" tears began to Glisson in her dark brown eyes "I've never been on a carriage ride before and I've only seen them in fairy tales, but I believe the carriage ride with you was my very favorite moment, William." Hattie could feel her father watching them, so she knew William would not kiss her again, so she hugged him tightly and whispered, "I hope I dream about you tonight, dancing in your arms and saying goodnight, with a kiss." Hattie pulled away, and with a calm voice said "Goodnight William. I'll see tomorrow!"

"I look forward to having such lovely company, young lady." Mr. Marshall reached over to shake Adam's hand. "Goodnight Adam, I'll send my man over tomorrow around four for Hattie. Thank you and your lovely wife for letting me steal her away on Christmas Eve. I promise to have her in church by seven.' He reached over and patted Hattie's face lovingly "Goodnight princess, sleep well and pleasant dreams!"

Hattie watched the man that had stolen her heart climb up next to his coachman and drive away.

Chapter 19

"Grandma, I just read Aunt Hattie's diary and I wanted to share what she had to say one year after her friend's disappearance. I just had a hunch she might try to see that old mansion again on Christmas Eve and I was right." Hattie felt excited with her latest clues found a year after the Marshall's had disappeared. Now that William was her dear friend, her need for solving the mystery was even greater. "May I read it to you before you get busy with your cooking?"

"If it means that much dear, I'll take the time." Nettie walked over and joined her granddaughter on the bed "Lands sake Hattie, what time did you get up? It's still dark outside."

"I couldn't sleep grandma. This mystery is weighing heavy on my mind and mama and daddy still haven't given me permission to go with William tonight to find out what's in that attic." Hattie opened the diary "Grandma, maybe you could put in a good word for me before they leave for work. It will be three o'clock before they get home and William is sending a car for me at four."

"Hattie darling, I cannot interfere with your parent's decision. It's not my place to voice an opinion." Nettie felt bad for her anxious granddaughter so she gave her a loving hug "Cheer up pretty girl, they haven't said no yet." Her old hand touched the diary "Why don't you read Hattie's words and get your mind off the decision right now. Everyone will be expecting their breakfast soon."

"Alright grandma, we mustn't make them mad first thing." Hattie looked down at the words and started reading.

December 24, 1815   Dear Diary, another year has gone and I still miss my friend terribly and think about her every day. I just went through the motions today, cooking Christmas Eve breakfast, then lunch, then supper, with mama. She chatted the day away, but I must admit, I didn't hear anything she was saying. My mind was on last Christmas Eve, the very last time I saw Pattie. In my mind, I relived going to the mansion just as it was growing dark, to give Pattie her Christmas present. That's when I heard piano music coming from the house and had a small glimpse of hope that everything was alright.

Joan Byrd

When I knocked on the door, everything fell silent and daddy told me I properly just heard the wind blowing through the oak trees, but diary, I know I heard someone playing the piano, O Holy Night. Daddy didn't see the glow from the attic window either, nor the horrible thing with glowing red eyes. Staring at me.

Dear Diary, I did a very foolish thing tonight and could have gotten myself into danger, but God's protecting angel had to be with me to see that I got home safe. Not being able to sleep, I slipped from the house around 11:00 p.m., after everyone had went to bed. At the barn, I saddled Star and road out to the Marshall Mansion. Diary, my heart still pounds when I recall what I saw and heard inside that abandoned house. The moon had slipped behind clouds, making it clear for me to see lights coming through the cracks of the closed shutters and underneath the front door. Walking up on the porch, I could hear someone singing as the piano played O Holy Night and I recognized my friend's lovely voice. Pattie had sung that song on Christmas Eve, 1813 and suddenly my heart grew happy as I thought, she's alive, Pattie's alive. I assumed My daddy was right when he said they were probably called out of town, but now they had returned.

Then I wondered why Pattie had not come by to let me know she was home, it wasn't like her. Then I brushed that thought from my mind and just rejoiced for my friend's return. I knocked happily on the door, expecting to hear the footsteps of Mr. Rockford, the butler. Instead, the house grew dark and so still it gave me the willies. I backed off the porch slowly, afraid to breathe and that when I saw the glow from the attic. I raced out to where I left Star and climbed in the saddle. I could still see the light glowing and it grew brighter as midnight approached, then I saw it, looking out. But not at me this time. Something on the side of the house had the hideous things attention. I looked in the direction it was staring and saw a tall man wearing a long dark wool coat and shiny boots, his eyes on the evil apparition. It was a though they were communicating with one another in spirit talk.

Being afraid of getting caught by the man, I took the reins tightly in my hands, ready to go slowly and silently away, when Star gave a wenny, and shivered as though he could sense the danger around us. The man looked straight at me and I instantly recognize him. It was William Marshall.

I turned Star around and raced down the hill, and straight home. I never intend going back to that mansion Dear Diary. There's something strange going on behind those shutters and that thing in the attic is something straight from hell. I just pray I can sleep this night and not have bad dreams about that mansion, that demon, or Mr. Marshall. Hattie Russel.

"Heavens, child, are you sure you want to go to that mansion tonight?" Nettie shivered "Your Aunt Hattie was real scared and declared she would never set her foot there again. If that things still in that attic, Lord help us."

"That's why I have to go grandma, me and William! That demon is not the only spirit inside that old house. I believe, with all my heart, that Pattie, her mother, and all the staff are trapped inside and their souls cannot get out, until someone sets them free." Hattie closed the diary and followed her grandma down to the kitchen to fix breakfast for all those leaving for work. "Don't you see, Aunt Hattie chose me to find Pattie and That's where I'll find her, Aunt Hattie said so herself. When she got there that night, she saw the house was alive with lights and she recognize her friend singing O Holy Night." Hattie poured orange juice for her family as she continued.

"The exact same thing happened on Christmas Eve 1814, the year they all vanished. Aunt Hattie heard someone playing the piano, O Holy Night. She couldn't see the lights coming from the cracks in 1814 because the moon was full and it cast it bright light on the house. The trees were small then, so it had a clear shot down on the mansion."

"What do you make of William Marshall showing up for that one night and wearing the exact outfit as your friend William?" Nettie could tell her granddaughter was trying to sort out the coincidence of her friend dressing in the same outfit as his great-great- grandfather. "Perhaps your friend just admires that style Hattie. It's not too far- fetched. I wouldn't be worrying baby girl."

"You are right grandma, lots of men like boots in the winter and a wool coat never goes out of style." Hattie thought to herself, "Are you trying to convince grandma or yourself? I shall ask him when the time is right." Hattie's attention was drawn to her parent's coming in the kitchen. She took the plate of fried bacon and sausage from her grandma and carried it to the table.

"Mama, did you and daddy decide if I could go to the mansion with William tonight?" Hattie whispered, not wanting her brothers to hear, especially Matthew, who would have a cute remark about it. "Please tell me I can go mama, it's the only way I can solve the Marshall's disappearance and William has given me permission to go with him!"

"Oh Hattie, I'm just not sure it would be the right thing to do. You barely know Mr. Marshall, and his sudden interest in you has me worried." Carolyn pulled her over to the side, so the boys could eat their breakfast and not listen to their words "Darling, I'm not sure what Mr. Marshall is planning and you are so young and innocent you see him as a good friend."

"He is a good friend mama, my very favorite friend and I trust him, with all my heart!" Hattie was smart enough to know what her mother was referring to, so Hattie whispered even lower "William would never touch me in the wrong way, mama. He is not a pervert desiring sex with a ten-year-old girl. William is a true gentleman and he wants this mystery solved just as much as me and Aunt Hattie."

"Carolyn, I think Hattie has a point." Adam had walked up to join the conversation, leaving Gideon and Nettie to keep the boys occupied. "I know Hattie and William's relationship is somewhat strange, but I think they genuinely love each other. Something tells me we should trust our daughter and let her go with Mr. Marshall tonight."

"Oh, thank you daddy!" Hattie turned to her mama "You can trust me mama. God has given me the common sense of a detective and I can read people and know if they're good or bad."

"Then, if you go, dress warm and please be careful Hattie." Carolyn hugged her daughter tightly "I wouldn't forgive myself if something were to happen to you."

"William will be with me mama and most important, God's angels will be beside me." Hattie made a face "As long as Theodore Johnson isn't along for the adventure, I'll be fine."

"Not your favorite person, sweetheart?" Adam rubbed the top of her head "Andrew said the butler took them home from the dance and he stared at them in the rearview mirror the entire drive home."

"Mr. Johnson is bossy, demanding and he never smiles!" Hattie felt light as a feather with joy "Why William puts up with the hateful man is beyond me."

"Then let's hope the delightful butler stays at the rock cottage, out of my girl's hair." Adam laughed and hugged her, then went to eat quickly, before heading out to milk, and helping out at the cookie factory on their last Christmas sales day.

"We'll let you go, sweetheart, but have Mr. Marshall bring you home right after you investigate that scary old house!" Carolyn took Hattie's face in her hands "You will not be spending the night with that man, understand?"

"Yes mama, I'll have William bring me home just as soon as the mystery is solved."

"Well, I must eat my breakfast and get ready to go." Carolyn walked with her to the table, which was almost vacant. All her sons except for Andrew had gone out to help milk. He had hung back to hear their decision on Hattie's going or not. Carolyn picked up her fork and began eating as she continued her talk "You will be gone when we return dear. The store closes at three, but it will take a while to clean everything before we can leave."

"Mama. I'm not feeling good about this at all." Andrew looked over at his sister who was trying to eat and listen to what her brother was saying. "Mr. Marshall is old enough to be Hattie's grandpa and he acts as though they are courting."

"Would you care to explain why you feel that way Andrew? Has Mr. Marshall done anything inappropriate to this girl?" Carolyn looked from Andrew to her daughter, trying to read her.

"For one thing, he asked me to call him William because we would soon be family."

"Did he? How odd." Carolyn looked at her daughter "Hattie, do you know what Mr. Marshall was referring too?"

"William is very religious mama, despite what Libby Fisher thinks." Hattie defended her friend and hoped Andrew's comments did not alter her mama's decision about her getting to go to the mansion "He has paintings of Mary with the baby Jesus and one of Jesus, hanging on the cross. I noticed an old worn bible lying on the side table beside his chair. I can guarantee it's not Theodore Johnson's."

"Can you explain why your date had this Theodore Johnson take me and Shannon home then, after the dance last night?" Andrew didn't want to spoil Hattie's chances of going to the mansion to solve her mystery, he just didn't trust Mr. William Marshall alone with his little sister.

"I think William wanted to make me feel special, like a real date. So, he took me home, wrapped in a warm blanket and his protecting arms. Then he poured us two cups of hot chocolate, loaded with marshmallows." She smiled up from her plate "He was a perfect prince, making me feel like a princess, nothing more."

"Not even one little kiss, kid-o?" Andrew reached over and hugged her.

Hattie blushed remembering the very grown up kiss from William, but she knew not to divulge that information, it was her secret and happy memory.

"Of course, my date kissed me goodnight, same way as daddy" Hattie sighed "Such a gentleman." Hattie smiled at her brother "And did you kiss your date goodnight, like daddy kisses me?"

"She got you Andrew." Carolyn laughed then stood up, eyes on her daughter "Just remember what I told you Hattie and do not take any chances with what's ever in that attic. Make sure Mr. Marshall is with you at all times."

"And keep an eye out for him as well." Andrew got up "Darn, I wished I was going to watch out for you."

"I'll be with William, so I will be fine Andrew." Hattie got up to hug her brother and mother "Besides, William said we had to go alone if we were going to solve the mystery."

"I'll see that Hattie dresses warm, Carolyn." Nettie walked over to see them off "I will also have Hattie to call her friends whom she invited to go with her tonight and explain why they couldn't go."

"I know what they will say grandma." Hattie remembered her friend's faces when she told them about the demon in the attic. "I'm sure Jane, Amy, and Bobby have all come up with good excuses as to why they cannot go with me." Laughing, Hattie ran up to find Aunt Hattie's present to take with her to the mansion.

Chapter 20

Hattie heard the car pull in the front and looked out to see Mr. Theodore Johnson climbing from the driver's seat. She made a face as her grandmother made her way to open the door to the unsmiling man.

"I'm here for Miss Russel madam." His attention fell coldly on Hattie, who stood waiting behind her grandmother holding a big bag. "There you are!" he started to take the bag from her and she pulled it close to her chest. "The bag child, I shall store it in the trunk for you."

"That's alright Mr. Johnson, I think I'll just keep it in the back seat with me." Hattie forced a smile "It's no trouble, really sir."

"Then you may store the bag in the back seat, Miss Russel, but you will be riding up next to me, so I can keep my eye on you." The butler bowed to Nettie politely, then stood aside for Hattie to walk out. He opened the back door and motioned for her to place the large bag inside, then he shut the door, and opened the passenger door for her. Turning to the woman standing at the door, he nodded "We shall see your granddaughter home tonight Mrs. Russel. Good day!"

"Good day to you Mr. Johnson and happy Christmas!" Nettie called and noticed him tense up as he climbed in the big car and sped away with her granddaughter inside. "Dear Lord in Heaven, please keep that child safe tonight!"

The ride was quiet for most of the way until they were getting closer to town and Mr. Johnson rolled his eyes over on Hattie.

"What are you hoping Mr. Marshall will give you young lady? The painting perhaps, his home or the mansion on the hill?" a harsh laugh came from his lips "Or are you hoping for everything he owns, just a little gold digger?"

"I assure you Mr. Johnson, I am nothing of the sort!" Hattie detested this man's attitude and she couldn't wait to be out of his company. "I don't expect William to give me anything but his loving friendship and a chance to solve the mystery."

"For your own good, as well as Mr. Marshall's, I suggest you forget solving the mystery on the hill." He stared coldly ahead as he drove down the hill to the cottage.

"That sounds like a threat Mr. Johnson!" Hattie was glad she would soon be with her friend and away from this strange man "Do you know something about the mansion you would like to share with me?"

He stopped the car just outside the cottage door and turned to face Hattie, anger shooting from his eyes "I know enough to tell you it is not safe to nosey around that place where strange things happen to snooping people."

"What sort of things? Things like mysteriously disappearing?" she climbed out and retrieved her bag from the back seat, then looked back through the open door "Are you hiding something up there and you're afraid we might find out what it is, sir?"

"You, Miss Russel, are an outspoken young lady! May I suggest you respect your elders as well as listen to their advice when given!"

"Perhaps I am outspoken when someone is threating me, Mr. Johnson, and I do respect my elders and listen to good advice offered when it comes from someone I can trust!" Hattie slammed the door and left Theodore Johnson fuming as she went to the front door and knocked.

"Hattie, where's the diver?" he looked to see the car sliding inside the outside garage "I told him to see you in before putting the automobile up."

"I got out before he could William." Hattie still felt weird about her conversation with the butler. "I didn't know Mr. Johnson was your driver too."

"Theodore? I don't understand Hattie. I sent Benson after you. Mr. Johnson ask if he could have the evening off, so I gladly said yes." William took her hand and led her inside "What's in the bag?"

"William, I don't know what happen to Mr. Benson, but Johnson picked me up and he wasn't polite at all!" Hattie noticed her friend's face grow pale as she spoke "He warned me, warned us to stay away from the mansion tonight. He same as threaten me that if we went, something would happen to us."

"Theodore can be very dramatic Hattie." Mr. Marshall walked her to the sitting room and took her coat "I'm truly sorry if he frightened you sweetheart. I wanted your evening to be as special as you are, not hindered by Mr. Johnson's ravings."

"I'm here now, with you William." Hattie looked around, hoping to see a Christmas tree or a least some decorations on the mantle. "William, don't you put up any decorations at Christmas? Sleepy Creek is known for the elaborate decorations on every building and house and there's not one candle glowing in your home."

"Would that please my girl?" William reached over and touched her face "Maybe I can get Theodore to put up one small tree."

"One small tree is better than nothing, William." Hattie smiled "Christmas should be a joyful celebration, it's our Lord's birthday."

"You are right Hattie, love came to earth on the first Christmas when God sent us the gift of His son." William turned around when the door opened and Theodore Johnson walked in. "Theodore, would you care to explain why you picked up Hattie when I sent Benson?"

"Quite so sir, I picked up the little up-start when Benson suddenly grew ill and I offered my services." The butler's eyebrow arched up "I had to forego my time off to help out a fellow servant."

"That was very charitable Johnson, but it did not give you the right to scare my girl." Mr. Marshall watched him closely. "First, you owe Hattie an apology, then you can get a Christmas tree and put it up in here while we are having our dinner. You'll find lights and ornaments in the attic."

"Which attic, sir? The one in here or the one in the 'shut off' mansion?" Johnson knew he had struck a cord with the wealthy man staring at him "Yes, that's what I thought, 'sir'. This house has never had an ornament placed in it, nor will it ever."

"William, are you going to let Mr. Johnson boss you around?" Hattie's distaste for this rude man was growing stronger "Why should he say what can and cannot be done in your home?"

"Yes William, tell the child the truth." The butler sneered "If you expect to take her up to your mansion, the truth will have to be told."

"What truth William?" Hattie started to worry about her friend's honesty "Tell me what?"

"Theodore, just go see if the cook is finished with our dinner and leave Hattie along." His eyes fell on hers "I'll tell her everything in due time Johnson. You just need to leave. Take the reminder of the night off! Forget the tree! Just do as I said, then leave!"

"Very good sir." Theodore Johnson looked pleased with himself as he started for the kitchen door, then turned "Have fun tonight, I know you will." He smiled at Hattie and disappeared behind the door.

Hattie looked up, questions lacing her big brown eyes "William, should I be afraid of you and what you might do to me?"

"Hattie, darling…" his fingers brushed over her lips "I could never hurt the one I love most. Please don't let Theodore's cold words upset you. He is jealous over my affection for you." Standing up he took her hand "Let's not let Johnson destroy our beautiful night together, my dear Hattie." He looked down at the big bag "Perhaps you can tell me what you brought in the bag, while we dine."

Hattie's smile was shaky as she walked with William to the small cozy dining room, lit only by candles. Helping her sit down, William walked over and picked some greenery off a potted plant and placed some leaves around the candle holders.

"There, my darling, a little- Christmas decorations to brightened up our table." Hattie saw the same love reflecting in William's eyes that always warmed her heart and she knew if there was something that needed telling, he would share it with her.

"That's beautiful William, thank you." Hattie reached over and took his strong hand "I won't pressure you in telling me what Mr. Johnson was talking about. I know, if there's something I need to know, you will tell me."

"Hattie Russel, you are so wise for someone so young. If only…" He stopped when the server came in with the food. Smiling, the woman walked over to a small bar and poured two glasses full, then set them in front of the diners and left the room. "I hope you don't mind my dear. I took the liberty to order you another sherry since you like it at the club house. Just sip it with your food and you want get dizzy."

"Thanks William." She took his hand and bowed her head "Heavenly Father, thank you for this lovely meal and wine. Thank you for my William, whom I will love forever. Amen." Looking up at him, she saw a warm smile on his handsome face. "William, what was you going to say before the maid came in with our dinner?"

"Oh, Hattie, how can I explain my feelings for you when I don't understand them myself." He picked up his glass and took a drink before continuing "Hattie, I…I don't just love you, I'm in love with you. Do you know the difference?"

"I think my gift to you will prove I know the difference William." She stood up "May I go get it, I don't think it can wait another moment?"

"By all means Hattie, get it and show me!" he watched her walk swiftly to the sitting room and took a relieved breath when she stepped back in the dining room carrying the big bag. "That is a very large bag dear Hattie."

"That's because there's two gifts inside it. One for you William, and one from my great-great-Aunt Hattie, to her dearest friend in the entire world, Pattie Marshall." Hattie held out the box wrapped in the old red paper and mashed white bow "You know William, it never dawned on me before, but this is the exact same paper you gave me."

"Just a coincident pretty girl. Red and white are two Christmas colors, right?" William Marshall held out his hand toward the bag containing his present "May I? I'm dying to know what you made for me."

Hattie pulled out the box, almost the same size as her aunts, only hers was wrapped in a white paper with a green and red bow gracing the top.

"I hope you like it William. I had to wait for the paint to dry before I could wrap it." Hattie's hands trembled as she passed him the beautiful package.

Slowing he took off the wrappings and opened the lid. Looking down, William Franklin Marshall gasp at what he saw looking up at him.

Chapter 21

"Hattie, is that you and me, in the future?" tears formed in William's eyes as he gazed down at a painting of him and an older Hattie, in each other's arms.

"Do you like it? "Hattie held her breath as William continued to stare at the perfect likeness of him and herself around twenty.

"Like it, Hattie, I love it darling." Holding the painting with one hand, he reached over and pulled her next to him "Does this mean that you feel the same way about me? I could only dream of a life with you, my dearest. A life where I would wait for you to grow up and I could ask you to be my wife."

"William, dearest, that would take a miracle. When I'm twenty, you will be eighty. That would never change my deep love and affection for you, but how William?' Hattie touched his face "Your age hasn't shown on your handsome face yet, but William, you can't expect to stay young forever."

"If you believe that darling, why did you paint me looking just as I do now and not a much older man?" his eyes held hers.

"Because William, that's the face I first saw looking down at me when you bought that cookie at the market." Hattie couldn't understand why she had fallen in love with William, but she did and needed for him to know "I dream about the kiss on the carriage William and I feel like a grown woman in a child's body. I know it might sound funny coming from a child William, but I am in love with you."

"Hattie, it doesn't sound any more, funny than a grown man declaring his love to such a young girl, but I cannot deny my feelings for you and…" he took her hand and walked inside the sitting room "and I cannot lie to you anymore about myself."

"So, this is the truth I need to know?" Hattie felt nervous about what he was going to tell her, but she had to know "Whistling water melons William, please tell me!"

William smiled, still seeing the young Hattie come out, then he got serious "Hattie, what I am about to tell you might make you despise me, even hate me, but it must be told."

"William, you are scaring me." Hattie reached for his hand "Whatever it is, it can never change my love for you. Please believe that."

"I pray it won't darling." William Marshall took a deep breath "Hattie, I lied about my age, I am forty years old."

"Forty? But that's a good thing, isn't it William?" Hattie sit up "That will make you forty-eight when I reach eighteen, then we can be married!"

"Hattie, darling." William stood up and walked over to the mantle "The truth is, I would still be forty when you reached eighteen, even twenty." He closed his eyes, trying to blot out what he had to say next "I will be forty when you are eighty, my darling Hattie."

"William, I don't understand. How could you possibly not age?" Hattie joined him at the fireplace "Please, tell me how?"

"I became forty on January the first, 1815 and I have remained forty." William reached for Hattie when she grew dizzy from his revelation "Hattie, I'm really two-hundred and forty years old. I am not William Franklin Marshall the forth, I am William Franklin Marshall, the only one."

"That's why you dress the way you do. Your age hasn't changed and neither has your wardrobe. You chose to live here instead of the mansion because you are afraid what you might find inside."

"My little detective is close to the truth." Mr. Marshall pulled her over to the sofa and gently lowered her. He placed his arm around her. "Hattie, I'm not proud with what I done to my family. If I could take it back, I would. I begged with that demon to take me and release them, but it was too late darling. I'd...I'd already sold my soul to the devil in exchange for eternal life. I had become a mad man, obsessed with dying like my father and grandfather. He pushed me and edged me on, telling me that soon he would have me and I would burn forever! I... couldn't understand, I had been a Christian, devoted to my wife and the apple of my eye, my little girl, my Pattie."

"Christmas Eve, 1815, it was you that Great-great- Aunt Hattie saw conversing with the thing in the attic window!" Hattie sat up, the truth dawning on her in every direction "Theodore Johnson is one of them, isn't he? He couldn't have become your butler when you were ten, unless...he was your butler when you were really ten,

111

in the late seven-teen-hundreds." Hattie wiggled out of his embrace and stood up, pacing the floor as reality struck her "No, he wasn't your butler when you were small, he was your butler when you moved to Sleepy Creek! No wonder Johnson spoke British, he talked that way before! Aunt Hattie heard him and said he like to tell jokes, especially to Mrs. Folly, the cook! Theodore Johnson and Mr. Rockford are the same man, or shall I say demon?"

"Hattie, you frighten me how you can see the truth!" William joined her and pulled her around "Hattie, he's dangerous! He is the one who drove me into giving my little girl to that monster! The gift I gave her to open on Christmas Eve, the one I told her would be with her forever! He was waiting for her to open it on Christmas Eve, after dark. Rockford told me to hide it in the Attic, so she could find it, like a hide and seek game. I told them I had to go to the office for something. I had to get out of the house, or I would have been trapped inside too. I waited outside, waited and watched to see the light glowing from the dreaded thing when it came out and got my…little Pattie." Tears fell down William's cheeks as he remembered the horrible night.

"The beast was supposed to go down stairs and consume everyone in the house, but something stopped him. I saw him looking out the window at Hattie as she rode away on the back of her daddy's wagon as though he were the one trapped, trapped inside the attic. I waited outside, seeing light from underneath the front door, but only silence. The shutters had slammed shut when the box was opened and I could hear the doors being locked from the inside. The only key was in my pocket and I knew if I dared to go inside, the devil would drag me down into the pits of hell." William walked up to the painting and touched his daughter's face.

"Hattie, I killed her, the need to live took my daughter from me! The one thing I loved most!" he looked at Hattie for understanding "I stayed until one o'clock, that's when the glow in the attic faded away. I came back on Christmas night, hoping to find it gone so I could go in and save my family and staff. But the light was back and so was the thing, on the strike, of midnight."

"It was the cross! The cross that Aunt Pattie hung around your daughter's neck!" Hattie remembered the precious gift given to her friend to protect her from harm "The cross was made from the dogwood tree, same as the one Jesus died on! That demon saw

Pattie's cross and it froze him so she could run from the attic and lock him inside!"

"Oh, sweet girl, I pray you are right! That thing could not torment them forever, but they still were trapped inside that house. They must have starved to death or froze when the firewood gave out." William sank down in his armchair weeping. "How can I make it up to them? They're gone and there's no way that I will ever see them again."

"You can see them in heaven." Then reality hit her again "William, if you can't die, except when our Lord comes back, you might never see them! You said you sold your soul to the devil." Hattie grabbed his hands and got down in front of him "Start praying William, pray real hard and ask God to forgive you! Ask Jesus for another chance! Help me save their souls, William, your family, your staff! They are trapped inside that mansion and we gotta get them out, so they can go to heaven."

"If I go inside, my dearest, he will suck me down and all that will be left is my dust!" William pulled her into his arms.

"Then I will go inside myself William, but you must promise me, you will not run away this time." Hattie looked at him with pure love on her young face "You must be there for me William, if you love me. If I get trapped inside that house, you must open the door!"

"I have never loved anyone like I do you Hattie. Fate has played an evil trick on us and we were born years apart." William held her tightly "You can count on me Hattie. I will never forsake you darling. I will be waiting just outside that door and I will face the devil himself if he tries to harm you, my beloved! I promise you, I will not let you down!

Joan Byrd

Chapter 22

Hattie and William slipped in the back pew when they reached the church for the Christmas Eve service. Her mother had been looking for her and smiled when her daughter waved from the back of the church. William had told her they might need to slip out so they would have plenty of time to go to the mansion before midnight, the time the monster was released from its box in the attic. Hattie had written a note for her mother telling her about the early dismissal and she would slip it to the usher in the back of the church to give to Carolyn Russel after the service.

The time had come to leave. It was ten o'clock, giving them only two hours to drive there and make their last plans before Hattie went inside the old mansion. Un-be-known to them was the boy hiding in the shadows as they left the church.

Bart Brower smiled and hopped on his electric bike and followed behind them, knowing they would be going to the old mansion on the hill. As he rode along, he thought "Little detective, I will crack that mystery before you and be the headlines in tomorrow's paper." He laughed out as the wind whipped through his red hair. "Hattie will chicken out when she sees that old house in the dark, with only the moonlight to show her the way." Bart chuckled as he turned in the long drive way leading to the secluded mansion, nestled under the large oak trees. "She's a girl and girls are afraid of their shadow, not to mention all the spiders I'll warn her about them waiting to jump on her when she goes inside."

William pulled the car in front of the house and turned to face the young girl who had stolen his heart. He reached over and brushed his fingers over her lips.

"Hattie, it would be so easy to take you and leave this place right now. Wait until you are old enough to marry me and run away with my new bride and live happily ever after." William's voice came tender "My heart is so full of love for you darling, I long to hold you in my arms and…make love to you." His gaze fell on the house "But I must do what is right and face the fact that our time will soon be over."

"William, is there no other way? Couldn't we still save all those trapped inside and have a life together after I'm grown?" Tears rolled down her sweet young cheeks "I don't want to lose you William."

"My beloved, it will kill me to leave you, knowing your love for me is the same as mine, but I must stop thinking about myself and what I want." Tears, to match Hattie's fell down his face "My little Pattie needs me, Hattie. Susanne and my loving staff have suffered far too long because of my choice to live forever."

"I know you're right William. It's the thought of never seeing you again on this earth that breaks my heart." Hattie reached for his hand, twice her size, lifted it to her lips and kissed it. "William, did you love Susanne the same way you love me?"

"I have never loved anyone, not even Pattie, more than I do you Hattie." William pulled her into his arms "Growing older and dying young was not the only thing that drove me mad in 1814. Susanne had asked me for a divorce a few weeks before Christmas and said she would be taking Pattie. I never seen it coming. She had fallen in love with our lawyer and told me I had been too busy for her or our daughter."

"Oh, William, I'm so sorry. It would have broken your heart to lose your daughter." Hattie looked at the clock on the dash, it read ten-thirty. "William, any last- minute instructions before I go inside?"

He climbed out quickly after he checked the time and walked around to help Hattie out, then he reached in the back seat for Pattie's Christmas gift Hattie insisted they bring. He walked her to the porch and placed the big key in the lock and turned it, then removed it, out of precaution.

"Now listen to me Hattie, check your watch and if it draws close to twelve, get out of that house."

"William, I been thinking about how to get everyone out and I think I know the answer." Hattie swallowed "I have to get that box out of the attic and bring it outside before midnight."

"Hattie darling, that is very dangerous, for you and the other souls in the house, if indeed they are still there instead of heaven." William pulled her close "Hattie, I lost Pattie because of that demon from hell, but I cannot lose you, my dearest, to him!"

"Don't you see William, it's the only way to rid that house of

115

'it' forever! As long as that thing is inside that attic, no one in Sleepy Creek is really safe." Hattie looked up, the serious situation painted on her beautiful young face. "William, my time is running out! It cannot be any other day but Christmas Eve! That's when he was released so that's when he must leave!"

"Alright Hattie, everything you are saying makes sense, but listen to my words and do as I say, when you get to the door with that box, hand it to me! I will take it from there, understand?"

"But William, you said you couldn't come inside or the devil would suck you, strait down to hell, suppose just standing in the open door could be the same effect on you?" Hattie's eyes were big with fear. Not for herself, but for the man she had fallen in love with.

"I'll take that chance Hattie, I will not let anything happen to you as long as I have breath in me!" William reached down and kissed her lips tenderly "Now go darling and do not take any chances with your life. I'll be right outside, keeping a watch on the attic window. When you need me, call out..." He hugged her one last time. "I will be here Hattie, I promise."

"I know." Hattie returned his hug and opened the squeaking door and stepped slowly inside. The two-hundred-year-old house reek with a musty smell as cobwebs fell over the curtains and furnishings. Old smoldering logs in the huge fireplace, lie cold and black and the tables and chairs were covered with years of dust and mold. Her eyes fell on a dried up, Christmas tree, the decorations still in place, along with unused candles ready to be lit for one brief night of celebration. Over the mantle hung another painting of the Marshall's in happier times and brown garland, once alive and green, cascaded just below the mantle, held up by large red bows, faded over time.

Were her ears deceiving her or was Hattie hearing music coming from somewhere close.

"Could it be the music room that Aunt Hattie wrote about? Was that where I will find the ghost?" feeling a hand on her shoulder, Hattie gave a soft scream and jumped around, hoping it wasn't the demon from the attic. To her surprise, Hattie looked into the wide eyes of Bart Brower.

"Bart Brower, what on earth are you doing here? This place is dangerous!"

"Hattie, were you just playing...music?" he swallowed.

"No Bart! The music was coming from the music room and it stopped when I screamed!" Hattie frowned "How on earth did you find me?"

"I had several good clues, Miss Detective!" not hearing the music, he suddenly grew brave "My first clue came when I was in the Christmas Attic Shop with my sister, who was shopping for a gift for some boyfriend." Bart couldn't understand why Hattie smiled so big from that statement "Like I was saying, my first clue was overhearing your friend Amy talking to you on the telephone and she said, I'm sorry Hattie, I can't go with you tonight, our family is driving up to Aunt Easter's for a Christmas party." He smiled broadly as he continued "Then I had sis take me to the bookstore, pretending I wanted to look around but I was hoping I hadn't missed your call to Bobby."

"So, you ease dropped on our conversation!" Hattie checked her watch, it was eleven and she didn't have time for Bart's childish games. She secretly wished the ghost would appear and scare him away. "What did you hear Bart, I haven't all night! That demon will come out of his box at midnight and I for one do not wish to confront him."

"Nice try Hattie Russel, the girl with the muscle." Bart chuckled "I heard Bobby chicken out on you too! I also heard him say he didn't want to see the glow from the attic!" another cocky smile fell on his lips "He also ask you if you were going after the church services tonight, so I waited in the parking lot and followed you and Mr. Marshall out her on my electric bike."

"Did you see William outside?" Hattie checked her watch again "Bart, I'm serious, did you or did you not see my friend?"

"Dope! He probably got scared and left!" he noticed Hattie's eyes grow dark "Gee Hattie, he could be hiding out there somewhere. I'm just glad he didn't see me. He's strange!"

"Scared of him, Bart?" Hattie was getting nervous, time was ticking fast "He don't bite."

"You should be scared of him Hattie." Bart actually looked sincere "I wouldn't put my trust in him if I were you. I know we're enemies Hattie Russel, but I wouldn't want anything to happen to you." He suddenly realized how he was sounding, like he cared, so he laughed to hide his feelings "Who else could I compete with in the season games?"

117

Hattie and Bart were so busy talking, they hadn't noticed the smell of a fire burning and the sudden candle light that flooded the dark room. Looking around, both young people stood in shocked silence until a young sweet voice melted the stillness.

"Hattie! Hattie, you came!" turning toward the sound of the voice, Hattie and Bart saw the pretty blonde standing on the stairsteps, smiling down at Hattie. "It's been so long dear friend! I've waited and waited!"

"Hattie...who...what is that?" Bart backed toward the door "Let's get out of here! She's...a...ghost!" he ran over to the door and flew out, leaving Hattie alone with the appearance of Pattie's spirit.

"Don't be afraid of me my dear friend, I will never hurt you." She looked up the steps and shivered "But he will Hattie, he will lock you in here with us forever!"

"Pattie, I'm not afraid of you. I've come to help you and your mama and staff." Hattie felt the package in her hand from her Aunt Hattie. She walked over and handed it to the pretty young girl staring down at her as though she was the ghost. "Pattie, my great-great- Aunt Hattie ask me to give you your long-awaited Christmas gift she made you in 1814. She left her diary to me, the one you gave her, and she ask that I find you and save you. That's why I chose this night, Christmas Eve."

"What is your name?" Pattie reached for the gift "And could you tell me what year this is, I've lost track."

"I was named after my Aunt Hattie. I am Hattie Russel and I'm ten-years-old." Hattie checked her watch, time was running out so she must move faster "Listen Pattie, I must go to the attic before midnight and get that box."

"The evil box?" she raced down the steps and hugged Hattie "Please, you must not open the door! I have it locked inside and if it gets out, we all will be doomed!"

"Pattie, you're already doomed, trapped inside this house. If I don't get rid of that box, you might never go to heaven." Hattie felt sorry for frightening the already scared girl, but she knew even she would be trapped if she didn't rid the house of that box. "Pattie, Hattie must be wondering where you are and why you're not in heaven with her. She missed you until she died in 1894."

"The year child?" Hattie turned to see Susanne and the staff listening behind her. "Then go to the attic, before it's too late for you."

"It's 2014 Mrs. Marshall. You have been a trapped in here for two-hundred-years.' She moved passed Pattie and the young girl took her hand "I've got to go now Pattie, before it's too late."

"I'm going with you Hattie. The cross saved me before." She smiled remembering her friend's words "If he comes out, it might work again."

"Good, let's go! We've got fifteen minutes left!" Hattie turned to walk up the steps and ran into Theodore Johnson.

Chapter 23

"Theodore Johnson! Or is it Mr. Rockford?" Hattie knew the detraction was to slow her down, so she would be too late and the demon would be out of the box and waiting.

"Mr. Rockford? How could you possibly be here? We all seen you vanish into thin air when you tried to leave for help!" Susanne Marshall stared up at the man blocking the way from Hattie and her daughter "We assumed the order the demon told my daughter came true and anyone who tried to leave the house would be sucked down to hell! We all thought you were our hero, but here you are."

"Yes, here I am, Susanne Marshall." He sneered "Too bad you didn't have the time to divorce William before he trapped you inside this house."

"Mama, you weren't going to divorce daddy, was you? You loved him and he loved you!" Pattie turned to the evil smiling man on the steps "Who are you? What are you?"

"He is a demon and he tricked your daddy into trapping you in the house!" Hattie had to think of a way to get rid of this evil creature "Did you convince Mrs. Marshall to get a divorce as well with your cunning words?"

"Always the detective, right Miss Russel?" his smile gave Hattie the creeps "Yet you don't take advice when offered. Did not I tell you to stay away from the mansion, you would be in danger?"

"You don't scare me! I have the Lord on my side!" Hattie pulled out her cross from beneath her blouse and held it up toward him. Letting out a gasp, he pulled back. Pattie reached for her cross and held it up, causing the evil being to take deep breathes. Hattie started walking toward him, words pouring from her innocent lips. "In the name of Jesus, I order you to return to your master, Lucifer! GO!" with that, the demon vanished and Hattie raced up the steps to the attic. Looking at her watch, she had only five minutes left before the demon would be set free.

William Marshall checked his watch thirty minutes earlier when Bart Brower raced from the house, white as a ghost. Marshall stepped from the shadows and grabbed the frighten boy who let out a scream.

"Keep still, boy! What's the meaning going inside my mansion without my permission?" his eyes were dark and angry "If you have wasted Hattie's time, I have you arrested for trespassing, kid or not!"

"Sir,...Hattie shouldn't be in that mansion! It's haunted!" Bart could still see and hear the blonde girl that appeared. "I...I saw a ghost standing on the stairsteps and she was calling Hattie's name!"

"Tell me, young man, what did this girl ghost look like?" William's head was spinning with worry over the young girl he had fallen in love with. Seeing Bart Brower shaking and staring at the window, which was casting an earie glow from the attic, Mr. Marshall turned him to face him "Stop staring at that demon's light boy, and describe what you saw!"

"Demon?" Bart swallowed "Hat...Hattie was telling the truth!" he could see the tall man's anxious expression, so to get away from this scary place, Bart knew he had to tell all he knew to this man so he could leave. "The girl ghost was about my age, I'd say, ten, and her hair was blonde, her eyes, blue as a clear southern sky. Quite a looker, sir."

"Pattie." William spoke softly as his gaze fell on the house "Hattie was right, their spirits have been wondering around in that mansion for two hundred years." Loosing his grip on the snooping boy, Bart Brower fled to his bike and took off.

William Marshall checked his watch again, quarter till twelve. His heart beat wildly as he made his way to the front door and took out his key.

"Hattie, darling, please hurry! Your time is running out!" hearing voices inside, William pressed his ear up against the door to listen. "Johnson!" his hand trembled. "He's trying to stop Hattie from going to the attic for the box!"

William knew there was only one thing he could do to help his love, pray. Dropping on the porch floor to his knees, William Marshall poured out his heart to the only one who could defect the Devil.

"My Lord, I have committed the worse kind of sin! To have life eternal on this earth, I sold my soul to the Devil and the cost was my family and all my devoted staff. I sacrificed my Pattie, the light of my eye, for selfish reasons and now, I would gladly give myself to Lucifer, for the release of those I love!" tears flooded William's eyes as he looked up to heaven "Father, I do not deserve your forgiveness, but if there's a ray of hope for me, I pray, I plead to you, for forgiveness! There is an innocent child inside that house, Lord, and she is in great danger from Lucifer's demons! Please, cast away her enemy who blocks her path from the demon in the box! This man who tempted me into my wrong choice! He is a manipulator, who's cunning ways can trap any soul into making the wrong choices!

"What I did, I take full responsibility for and I shall except the decision you make for my immortal soul. I am in your hands, Lord. Please, Jesus, help Hattie. I love her with all my heart and I would gladly give up my life for her. I would gladly lay down my life for Susanne, my staff, my beautiful Pattie, and for the young girl who stole my heart! My most ardent prayer is, that one day my Hattie and I can be together forever. Amen"

William looked over at the house when he heard Hattie's voice speaking loudly, asking the Lord to remove Johnson from her way. He stood quickly and walked back to the door and placed the key inside the lock. Looking at his watch, he knew his girl's time was running out.

"Hattie, if you're not at this door in three minutes, I'm coming in, devil or no devil!"

After Pattie unlocked the door to the attic, Hattie made her way quickly to the glowing light and lifted up the warm box. It seemed to come alive in her hand as it vibrated and bounced around in her tight grip.

"Let's get this thing out of here now!" Hattie ran down the two sets of stairs carefully and reached the front door, she found it locked tight. She closed her eyes as the box grew hotter and hoped the man she loved was waiting on the other side of the locked door. "William, please open the door! It's locked and it won't open!"

Hearing the squeaking sound, Hattie knew the front door was opening. William held out his arms as the spirits watched in wonder.

"Hattie, the box, give it to me now darling!" he cried out and grabbed the box and threw it in the grown up rose garden. A relieved Hattie threw herself in his arms, William, you did stay!"

"I would never leave you helpless, Hattie. I love you." William Marshall saw Pattie standing, watching the unusual scene between her father and this young girl. Tears filled his eyes, seeing his daughter for the first time in two hundred years.

"Pattie! My sweet, sweet girl." He fell down on his knees "Pattie, I'm so sorry, daddy's so very sorry. I know I have no right to ask you to forgive me for what I did to you." He looked around at the others watching, Susanne, his wife, Mrs. Folly, the cook, The twins, Milly and Tilly Shields, their chamber maids, Rose, Velda, and Joyce Ann, their devoted personal maids, and the quiet gardener, Mr. Peppers. "What I did to each one of you. I can never repay you for all your suffering and being trapped for two hundred years while I lived, every day at forty-years-old." He looked down, a broken man "If it makes you feel any better, I was a miserable unhappy man for two hundred years until something happen to change all that." William Marshall's attention fell on Hattie and the love that radiated between them could be felt by each spirit watching.

"I found true love, from a child, young as the daughter I had given away for my selfish vanity. Hattie saved me from myself. No longer did I mope around, an angry, mean individual, uncaring for my actions to others, no matter how much I hurt them. Hattie suddenly became my world and I didn't want to lose her."

"Daddy, the man you described before you met Hattie, does not describe the loving father I knew." Pattie walked over and took around him "It was Mr. Rockford who changed you just like he changed mama and made her think she wanted a divorce from you. You did do all of us wrong, daddy, but you came back to help save us. Daddy, I've never stop loving you." Pattie looked into his dark eyes "I forgive you daddy, for everything."

"Pattie, baby, thank you sweetheart." William Marshall hugged his daughter, then he heard laughter rolling out behind him and Pattie screamed when the dark grotesque demon arose from the ground, its sharp teeth protruding from his deform mouth. William stood up quickly and shoved Pattie behind him as he reached for Hattie, pulling her out of harm's way.

"Leave them alone, you demon from hell! It's me you want, take me!"

"No! William, you cannot go with that monster! Please

William…" Hattie clung to him "Jesus will save us!"

"Don't listen to this stupid girl William Marshall!" Its voice came loud and gruff "This Son of God does not hear you anymore, foolish man! We heard you praying to this God who does not care about your welfare anymore, after you sold your soul to the master!" the beast came a step closer to William Marshall "You belong to the master, William Franklin Marshall and this JES…US will not save you!"

"My girl is not stupid, you, slimy creature from the underworld! Me maybe, for falling in your trap, but not Hattie Russel! She is the smartest young lady I have ever met, and I will fight to be with her as long as there's breath in me!' William Marshall was on the defense now, for Hattie, the girl he had given his heart to. So, if he had a heart that felt this much love, then he knew his God did hear him when he prayed and Jesus would save them, just like it did Hattie inside when she ordered Johnson away in Jesus name.

William saw the beast crawling closer, so he pulled Hattie in his arms and spoke softly "Hattie darling, call out to Jesus now, to send his angels to save us from Satan! You are pure and innocent darling, he will listen. It cannot be me, or Pattie, she's a spirit, it has to be from my dearest love."

"Alright William, step to one side and watch the love and power of the most, high God!" Hattie kissed him quickly, then looked up, blocking the ugly monster out of her young mind, she prayed

"Lord Jesus, please send your angels down to help us rid the world of this demon, who has been sent by Lucifer to destroy us, your children, your people!"

The demon began to laugh his hideous grinding mockery of the very idea of a mere child thinking God would hear her pitiful cries for help. Suddenly, his laughter gave way to whimpering, as he began backing away from an unseen force.

All those watching' were frozen in stunned silence as the forces of good were battling the forces from hell. The only words moaning from its deform lips were

"It's you! It's you!" as the ground shook and trembled, then cracked open, swallowing the beast in one quick movement, then sealing the whole shut for all eternity.

Everything grew silent as William and Hattie reached for each other's hand and stared at the spot the demon had been observing so closely. The wind grew silent as a mist formed on the ground and the figure of a man in a long white robe appeared. No one needed to ask who this angelic figure was, they just knew. It wasn't an angel who answered Hattie's call, it was the Lord Jesus, himself. He had come for His lost sheep.

Chapter 24

Andrew lay in bed, unable to sleep, his mind going back to the Christmas Eve service at church. He had invited Shannon Brower as his date and all during the moving service, they stole glances at one another. Andrew could vision her face and her beautiful eyes, glowing in the soft candle light that lit up the small frame church.

Then Andrew's thoughts fell on his little sister, remembering seeing her and William Marshall slipping out the back of the church holding hands. He sat up and climbed quietly from bed, not wishing to wake Peter who slept in the other twin bed.

Finding his way down the stairs, he went to the kitchen and switched on the light. Pouring himself a glass of milk, he sat down at the table. He could see the moon shining bright outside and wondered if Hattie was up at that scary mansion, alone with Mr. Marshall. The phone rang out, startling him. He glanced at the clock as he grabbed the receiver, eleven o'clock.

"Hattie, is that you?"

"Andrew" came a male voice "Hattie is alright at the moment. This is William."

"Mr. Marshall?" Andrew grew anxious "Where is my sister, is she with you, sir?"

"Hattie is inside the mansion Andrew." William waited for a response as he kept his eyes on the house. He had called Andrew when he grew concerned for the girl he loved, knowing she would be left on the hill alone after he departed this world. "Andrew, are you there?"

Andrew stared at the phone, suddenly frighten for his little sister. "Mr. Marshall, why did you let Hattie go inside that house alone?"

"I had no other choice, Andrew. I haven't the time to explain it to you now, Hattie will fill you in later. I will not let anything happen to her, she means far too much to me."

"Which brings up a question, Mr. Marshall."

"Make it brief Andrew, time is not on our side here." William wanted this call to end so he could give Hattie his full attention.

"On the carriage, you said to call you William, because we would soon be family." Andrew nervously hit the table with his fist "What did you mean?"

"Did you ask Hattie what I meant?" William knew explaining the real reason could set off this protecting brother.

"I did, and Hattie said that you were a good man of faith, she had seen religious paintings in your house and a worn bible, stating it had to be yours because she couldn't see Theodore Johnson having it."

Despite the situation, William Marshall laughed at her last statement. "Hattie is right about the bible belonging to me instead of Johnson. He wouldn't ever look at it and the only reason he tolerated the paintings was because of their worth." He thought about what Hattie had told her brother and he knew she was covering up the real reason William had stated that they would be family. "Hattie was referring to the family of God, Andrew, when we get to heaven with one another."

"Yes, that's what I assumed she meant Mr. Marshall." Andrew rose out of his chair, too nervous to stay seated. "Is that what you were referring to…William or was it something deeper?"

"Andrew, if I told you, you might find it hard to believe." William checked his watch and wished he could end this call and head closer to the house.

"Try me William, I consider myself a man with an open mind."

"Andrew, I cannot explain why it happened, but I fell in love with Hattie, not as the child she is but the woman she will become." William held his breath, hearing only silence on the other end "Andrew, Hattie feels the same way about me. She gave me a gift, a painting of us together, ten years in the future."

"You and my ten-year-old sister love one another?" he tried to wrap his mind around the ridiculous situation "She's just ten, how can you believe she isn't just fascinated with you, like one of her fairy tales?"

"Andrew, I haven't the time to explain any of this to you. Hattie could be in great danger if I don't get her out of that house before twelve midnight! That demon in the attic will trap the girl I love inside that old mansion forever."

"What are you saying? That is the glow that can be seen from the attic window? A demon?" Andrew started pacing the floor, the

Joan Byrd

need to help his little sister sweeping over him.

"Yes Andrew, you heard me. The thing is trapped inside his box somehow and can only come out on Christmas Eve at the strike of twelve!" William knew he needed to get to his point fast "Just listen and do as I say, for Hattie's sake."

"Okay, tell me and hurry! I'll do anything to help Hattie!" Andrew stared at his robe, he wouldn't take the time to get changed.

"I need you here for Hattie when I leave her, she mustn't be alone Andrew, up here in the cold night!"

What are saying, you will be gone? You can't leave my sister in that house with that demon, William Marshall!" Andrew reached for his daddy's truck keys hanging on a nail beside the back door.

"I will never leave Hattie alone while she's inside that house Andrew! I told you I love her! That girl is my life!" William took an anxious breath "I need you to come up here and be here for Hattie, Andrew. My girl will need you when I leave this earth for good! Don't ask, there is no time to explain. Hattie will tell you everything when I'm gone. She will be grieving Andrew, after watching her one true love disappear from her forever! She will need your support and love. Fate has played a cruel joke on us, being born years apart from one another. Maybe it was what I had done that I was being punished, but that does not explain why it happen to such a loving, pure, and innocent girl, like Hattie." Checking his watch, he grew with tension. "Andrew, please just hurry, and bring Matthew with you."

Matthew? Why him for God's sake?" Andrew wanted to leave at once, he didn't want to take the time to wake his childish bother and try to explain the situation to him."

"Your immature brother needs to grow up Andrew and learn to stop hurting his sister! She will need the support from all her family after I'm gone." William noticed the young boy running from the house and hearing the open door slammed behind him." Andrew, I've got to go right now! Just hurry!" with that, the phone went dead.

Andrew went quietly up the steps to Matthew and Thomas's bedroom. He slipped inside and put his hand over his brother's mouth, so he would not call out when he woke him. Pushing his arm, Matthew opened his eyes, they grew wide, trying to make out what was happening. Andrew bent low to his ear and whispered.

"Get your robe on and stay quiet, we need to talk." Andrew helped him up and waited for Matthew to slip on his robe and

128

bedroom slippers, then ushered him out the door and down to the lighted kitchen.

"Hey Andrew, aren't you a little old to be looking for Santa Clause?" Matthew chuckled.

"Get quiet moron, and listen to me, we have to go get Hattie up at the old mansion." Andrew knew his immature brother would have a cute remark about that.

"Going to spy on William and Hattie, big brother? Are you afraid he's raping our precious baby sister?" he joked and noticed Andrew's frown and serious expression "I know, it's the old mansion, sitting up there in the dark and that strange glow coming from the window! You want me to come along because you are scared of going by yourself, right?"

"Wrong, little brother!" Andrew grabbed his shoulders "Now listen, if it were up to me, I would have left you up there asleep in your bed and gladly went alone! Mr. Marshall insisted that I bring you!"

"Mr. William Marshall?" Matthew's eyes grew big "Why me? He doesn't even like me, Andrew!"

"Mr. Marshall believes you need a life lesson on growing up Matthew and there's something that could be happening as we speak that has our sister in grave danger."

"Hey, I'm grown up Andrew!" Matthew pouted

"Matthew, we both know you are nothing of the kind! You say things in a joking manner to people and it really hurts their feelings, little brother." Andrew escorted his speechless brother out the back door and to the truck. "Hattie needs her family tonight! She needs loving support and comforting, not some poor joke." Andrew stared ahead as he drove down the farm drive to the main road. He glanced over to a serious Matthew, staring out the window, questions racing through his young mind.

"Matthew, I'm not sure myself what's happening up there on that hill, all I know is, our little sister will be hurting from the loss of a man she really and truly cares about. Can you understand that much brother?"

Matthew looked over at his oldest brother, tears forming in his eyes. "I love Hattie too Andrew. I will do all I can to help my sister in whatever way she needs."

Andrew smiled and made his way quickly to the Marshall Mansion.

Chapter 25

Back at the mansion, Hattie watched as the spirits began their walk toward Jesus. Pattie Marshall touched Hattie's arm and smiled. "Thank you, Hattie, for saving our souls. Now we can go to heaven and our bodies, our bones, can be laid to rest in the church cemetery. You will find our remains huddled together in the music room where we starved to death before the Christmas season started in 1815. Our food ran out around April, 1815 and we had to burn broken up furniture after the wood ran out, just to stay warm." She noticed tears in Hattie's eyes as she talked, so she hugged her. "Thanks to you and daddy, our nightmare is finally over. Are there any questions you need to know before I depart with my Lord?"

"On Christmas Eve, 1814, Aunt Hattie said she heard a piano playing O Holy Night, coming from what she assumed was your music room. When she knocked on the door, the music stopped and everything grew silent." Hattie knew if she didn't ask her unanswered questions to Pattie Marshall, she would never know everything about the mystery on the hill. "A year later, Aunt Hattie returned and saw lights shining through cracks in the shutters and from under the front door. Then she heard the piano playing O Holy Night again, only this time, you were singing. She thought you had returned from a sudden family get-away and knocked on the door, expecting to hear evil Mr. Rockford coming to open it. She had no clue he was one of the demons and as before, the house became silent and the lights disappeared."

"Christmas Eve, 1814, Hattie did hear my mama playing O Holy Night while I went up to the attic to open my secret Christmas Present from daddy." Pattie looked over at her father, who was hanging his head as he listened to his little girl's story of the torment they suffered while he lived his life. "The reason everything grew silent was the cruse from the demon I had just released from the box in the attic. He had slammed shut the shutters and locked us inside this house the moment he came out. He said if anyone manage to escape from any entrance within the mansion, windows or doors, would be met by a demon and be sucked instantly down into the very pits of hell. That's what we thought happen to Mr. Rockford when he said he would go for help if he made it out alive.

The demon said we would come alive again every Christmas Eve unless someone from the outside tried to get in, then we would go back into our spirit world until the next Christmas. That's what happen when Hattie came the second time, the first time, when we were still alive, the beast froze our bodies until we were left alone."

"Pattie?" William Marshall walked up next to Hattie, with a question of his own "What happened in the attic that night to cause that horrible satanic monster to return to his box? I had been told he would be among all of you forever."

"I'm sure that was his plans daddy and all was going to his evil plan until he saw someone outside looking up at him."

"It was Hattie, she had come to bring you your Christmas present before her family went to the Christmas Eve church services. Not finding anyone at home, Hattie's daddy took her back to the wagon where her family waited and told Hattie, she had just heard the wind blowing and your family was probably called out of town on a family crisis. Aunt Hattie took one last look at the attic and she said there was something with red eyes staring at her, some sort of being." Hattie had often wondered why the demon was seen only at midnight on Christmas Eve, but her Aunt Hattie had seen it around seven p.m.

"I thought in my heart it must have been my friend Hattie and because she had drawn the beast's attention away from me for a minute, I snapped out of my frozen stupor and remembered the wooden cross around my neck, under my gown. Then words from Hattie came pouring back to me, like the Holy Spirit was speaking through her. I suddenly had hope that this gift of love from my best friend would protect me and everyone in the house, from that thing tormenting us while we were trap inside. When the thing turned to face me, I held up the dogwood cross. I told him my faith in the Lord Jesus would cast him back inside the box! Suddenly I felt something next to me. It brought me peace but only torment to the monster as he packed down inside the box and the lid fell shut.

Then I heard the spirit talking to me, he said: 'Get thee out, sweet child, closed tight the door to this attic, then lock it shut, for that demon, sent to torment you and this household, will be trapped in its walls. It can only come out of the box every Christmas Eve at the stroke of twelve, midnight, Christmas day, then return a short while after, casting his angry glow after dark. Go quickly, for even this night at twelve, it will crawl out for one hour before returning, finding himself locked in and no other demon can release him. Only someone from the outside, someone with a childlike love, one pure and innocent, can rescue you.'

Then I quickly locked the attic, placed the key in my pocket and started down the steps when the voice spoke one more time. He said: Know that I will never leave you Pattie. I am your guardian, given to you at birth. To keep you and the household from suffering while you live, your time will be cut short and even then, I will remain beside your spirit until the day my King and Creator takes you home, from whence you came.'" Pattie smiled a most beautiful smile, radiant and glowing as the Savior was holding out his arms to her. "I must go now Hattie." Pattie removed the precious gift from around her neck and handed it to Hattie, along with the painting of two best friends. "Keep these always Hattie Russel, to remember me and my dearest friend. I must go see Hattie, she has waited for me long enough. I'll tell her how brave her great-great=niece Hattie is and I know she will be proud of you for finding me and saving me." One last hug and Pattie Marshall joined Jesus forever, leaving William to say his farewells to the girl he loved so deeply.

"William, you can take five minutes to say goodbye to our Hattie." The voice flowed with love from the Lord's mouth as he watched the tender scene and waited.

"Five minutes?" tears began falling from Hattie's eyes as she clung to the man she loved so dearly "I will never see you again on earth, William! If I hadn't have insisted on solving this mystery, you and I could have had our life together!"

"Hattie, my sweet beautiful girl, we had to do the right thing and save my daughter and all those trapped inside the mansion. I could never let you make the same mistake I did two hundred years ago. Your heart has always been in the right place darling. You saved me and my soul my dearest Hattie. To lose you so soon after I found you hurts beyond words, but your entire life is ahead of you. I know you will morn my passing, perhaps all your earthy days. I can feel what you feel Hattie, our hearts were made to be one. I…" tears choked his words, as they fell uncontrollably down his handsome face "I love you Hattie Russel, with all my heart! To leave you like this, tears me into! If I could stay, I would and gladly, if I had the chance to start over and come back to you, I would welcome that Christmas miracle you spoke of."

"William." Came the loving voice "It's time."

"Oh, William, how can I tell you goodbye? How can I live without you?" Hattie threw her arms around his waist as he felt himself dying inside, not from the intimate death which waited, but by leaving his one true love.

"This is not goodbye Hattie sweetheart, this is just a brief parting until I see you again." He felt the Lord's hand on his shoulder "I'll see you in heaven, darling." With that, William Franklin Marshall was gone. Hattie bust into sobbing and through her tears she saw the loving face of her Lord, looking at her with the most incredible love she has ever witness. His words came in a still small voice as she heard him say: "Hattie, sweet child, grow in peace and filled with faith. You will find your love. It's meant to be." With those words of assurance, he was gone and she heard her brother call her name.

Hattie fell into Andrew's arms, weeping uncontrollable. She could not speak, for her young heart was breaking for the loss of her William. Andrew had seen the sad goodbyes between his sister and William and he knew his sister really and truly was in love with this man. He had hoped that Matthew felt the same passion and not make light of the situation.

"It's alright to cry Hattie. Shed as many tears as you need, we're here for you, me and Matthew." Hattie looked up at Andrew, who had tears in his own eyes.

"Matthew is here too? Did…did you see…William? He had to go to heaven, Andrew! How can I live without my William to share my life with? I truly love him, with all my heart!"

"We know you love him, Hattie." Matthew fell down in front of his weeping sister. "Never have I seen so much love between two people. I'm not sure what happen here, but I know William Marshall genuinely loved you Hattie."

"Loves me Matthew, he will always love me and I will always love him, until the day I die." Hattie suddenly realized her brothers were there so William had to call them to be there for her when he left. "My William called you, didn't he?" Hattie looked from Andrew to Matthew "He didn't want me to be left alone up on this lonely hill."

"William did call, he called me at eleven and said to come here for you." Andrew held tight to his sad sister "He cared about you kid-o and he does still love you. William will always love you Hattie."

"Thank you, Andrew, for believing in our love." Hattie reached for Matthew's hand "And thank you Matthew, for not making fun of me and saying I'm just a child living in a dream world."

"I'm sorry if I ever hurt you Hattie." Matthew gave his sister a hug. "Can you forgive me?"

"Matthew, my Lord ask me to grow in peace and have a strong faith." She touched his hand "I forgive you and I love you very much."

Hattie picked up the painting and felt the wooden cross around her neck, next to hers. She looked back at the last spot she saw William, sadness gripping her heart, then felt Andrew take her free hand.

"It's time to go home Hattie, there's nothing more we can do here tonight."

"Andrew, Pattie told me where we would find their remains and ask they get a proper Christian burial in the grave yard at church." Hattie looked back at the dark house, memories of her and William standing on the porch before she went inside. Feeling her tears returning, she asked Matthew to go lock the door and bring her the key, William's key.

"We will take care of Pattie's wishes Hattie, but for now, we need to get you home." Andrew watched as his sister walked over to William's car and look inside. She could still see them sitting there, pouring out their love to each other. She opened the door and breathed in the smell of his aftershave and pipe. Once again, Hattie broke down in sobs, calling out for her lost love.

Andrew could feel her great love and loss, as he too began to cry. He pulled her into his warm embrace and held her until the sobbing died down, then helped her to the truck and the two brothers took a very grown up ten-year-old home.

Chapter 26

The school gymnasium was bustling with Sleepy Creek citizens who had come out for the reading of William Franklin Marshall's last will and testament. Every person living in the small community had been given the day off, full pay, at the request of the town's founder. They all sat, chatting about the possibilities of receiving some sort of gift from the richest man in town. Everyone grew silent when the Russel family came in and was taken to the front row seat, where a large screen had been erected. Each drawn to their own emotions when they watched the young Russel girl weeping uncontrollable. They had heard of her closeness to Mr. Marshall and now they could see for themselves the stories were indeed true.

A distinguish man in a dark suit stepped out on a platform and looked out at the huge crowd.

"Good citizens of Sleepy Creek, it's good to see so many of you here today at Mr. Marshall's request. I represent Mr. Marshall, as his lawyer of sixty years, from the law firm of Dixon and Richards. Mr. Marshall has used our law firm in New York for many years, long before I took over from Mr. Dixon when he retired. My name is Kenneth Morris.

I have witness a big change in the man who practically owned this small town and it is all the doing of one young lady, who stole his heart. We will get to what William Marshall left her later, along with everyone sitting here this cold Friday morning, December 30. 2014. Like many people before Mr. Marshall, William ask if he could tell what he wished to give in his will himself. I met with Mr. Marshall a few days before Christmas Eve when he made the tape you are about to see. I ask that you refrain from talking during his message and if you have any questions afterward, feel free to ask me."

He motioned for the lights to be lowered and the tape to begin. When William appeared on the big screen, Hattie sat up and wiped her eyes as she whispered

"William."

His eyes fell down on Hattie, as if he had heard her. She smiled as he began "Dear friends" once again he looked at Hattie "My darling Hattie. I ask that you sit in that chair because it was there I was speaking so I could once again, looked into her beautiful brown eyes. You know how much I love you and that you are the joy that lights up my life, no matter where I'm at. I will save my last moments here speaking to you, my dearest, but I have a few gifts for the loyal citizens of Sleepy Creek.

I came to the run-down town two-hundred and forty years ago." Gasp came from those watching "I'm certain that statement must have taken most of you by surprise. I will not take the time to explain everything to you but have my girl to write it down for Mr. Mike Robinson, the Sleepy Creek Newspaper editor. For now, I think you will be pleased at the gifts you are about to receive from the oldest man in the town.

To all my employees at the Marshall Mills, I will have a trust made to keep the mill open indefinitely, as long as the town of Sleepy Creek is here. The new owner will see to it that your pay raises are made once a year and that each of you receive two weeks paid vacation days, along with your usual days off with pay, starting now." Excitement rose from the crowd and Mr. Morris raised up his quiet sign as Mr. Marshall continued

"I have set up a trust for both the school and the hospital, so that the buildings will always be kept up and the books and programs will continue. Teachers performing well will receive a bonus at the end of every semester, including a raise in their pay. Nurses and doctors will receive a pay raise every year as well as the hospital staff. Any new equipment needed will be supplied, to assure proper heath care for all our residents.

A college fund will be set up to help our young graduates go to the college of their choosing. I know Sleepy Creek is blessed with a lot of gifted and talented students who need just a little encouragement and the resources to help them fulfill their dreams. Follow your dream, young people. There's a big world out there just waiting. I know, I've seen most of it. But my happier moments are right here in the small town of Sleepy Creek. There are many other gifts that I have shared with you, dear friends, and you will learn about them later, but now, I need to move to the one who made those happiest moments for me, my Hattie.

Hattie Russel, you stepped into my life when I heard your sweet voice calling out, Hattie's Patties! It was the moment our eyes met for the first time that I gave my heart to you. I do not know why it happened, a man my age falling head over hills in love with a ten-year-old girl, but it did, and I will cherish that love for all eternity.

I leave to you my dear friend, my one true love, the girl that stole my heart, the rock cottage, with all the items inside it. It is where we found out we both shared the same love for one another and it will be there your fondest memories of us will be, my darling.

I leave to you the mansion on the hill and all its contents. My automobile, the carriage and everything inside the garage. I leave to you Marshall Mills, knowing they could not have a better owner and I know my loyal staff will work with the girl I love most.

I leave to you, my dearest Hattie, the club where we had our first dance and all the other businesses I own in Sleepy Creek. I leave you my wealth, which I have accumulated over the two hundred years I've lived along with the great wealth I started out with. I am worth billions my wonderful Hattie, and soon you will inherit all my wealth."

Hattie couldn't control her tears and she looked at the man she loved.

"I know my girl, and I know you are crying my darling. I understand what you are feeling and thinking. You are thinking, I would rather have you than all the wealth in the entire world. I would have gladly given up everything if it meant having you with me forever. My heart will forever be with you Hattie Russel. I love you!" Then he was gone and Hattie covered her eyes and cried.

The years seemed to go by quickly for Hattie Russel, even though her daily thoughts were consumed with William. She had reached the age of twelve when her brother Andrew became engaged to Shannon Brower. They had planned a June wedding in the small Methodist church and the Russel's unsure if the Brower's would except the marriage, they planned to hold the reception in the church's fellowship hall, following the ceremony.

Hattie volunteered to deliver the Brower family their invitations to both the wedding and the reception. Following the words Jesus had spoken to her on the night she had to say goodbye to her William, Hattie would go in peace, knowing she was not alone.

The Brower's were more than happy to hear what Hattie Russel had come to share with them. Ever since the Christmas holiday season began in 2014, the Brower's had witnessed this young girl's heart, thinking of others, like the Ashton family and saving Bart from a certain death. Their youngest son's confession of how he had followed Hattie and Mr. Marshall to the old mansion on Christmas Eve, the same year, and how he had plain to steal the credit for solving the Marshall mystery all by himself, he saw Hattie's bravery, while he himself was a coward and ran from the trapped people. They all considered Hattie Russel, a hero to the town of Sleepy Creek as did everyone in the small town.

Hattie had written the complete story involving the mystery of the Marshall's disappearance, just as William ask her to do, then delivered it to Mr. Robinson, the editor of the local newspaper. The owner of the Sleepy Creek Gazette was so impressed with Hattie's article, he wanted to print it in book form. With Hattie's financial support, Mike Robinson started the Marshall Publishing Company, and the Mystery of the Box in the Attic was an overnight success. Hattie also published Hattie Russel's Diary, 1814 and after combing through William's mansion, Hattie discovered a diary written by his daughter, Pattie. It was her day by day advents from the time they found themselves trapped inside the mansion. How they had to ration their food and how the gardener took seeds from varies fruits and vegetables, along with potato wedges, and with the soil from house plants, started growing food, so they wouldn't starve right away. In the winter when the fire wood gave out, Mr. Peppers started breaking up furniture. It's when the pump went dry, the end was obvious for the close group.

Pattie never forgot her best friend, Hattie Russel and mentioned her name in every entry. At one time, near the end of her life, when she was so weak she couldn't hardly write, Pattie Marshall penned these moving words:

Dear Diary, I don't think I can go on much longer. Mama died two days ago, and the twins followed, huddled together. Mr. Peppers and all our loyal maids, Rose, Velda, and my loving Joyce Ann, died hours apart, to weak to say goodbye. Mrs. Folly and myself are all that remain and I feel bad for the one that's left alone, with that horrible monster living in the attic. I must stay strong in faith and spirit and pray for the departure of dear Mrs. Folly, for I know my guardian is with me, even though I haven't heard his comforting voice sense that horrible Christmas Eve.

Dear companion, soon my hand will fall silent and the unwritten pages will remain white and bare. I do not know where my spirit will go, but I hope that I may go to heaven. My greatest fear is that I will be trapped in this house forever or until the young child my guardian spoke about, will come and save our souls.

Dear sweet blessed Savior, I do not know what my daddy did to put us in the horrible place, but knowing his heart, when he comes out of the spell the devil has cast over him, he will weep for me and mama, as well as the staff he cared so much about. I have never stopped loving daddy and I just need you to know, I forgive him.

The two things I have missed the most while being trapped inside my own home, is seeing my loving daddy's face and my dearest friend Hattie Russel. If you should see either of them before me, tell them how much I love them. Pattie Marshall, 1815

So, the wedding day came for Andrew and Shannon, along with the end of a long- time feud between the Russel's and the Brower's. At the reception, Hattie surprised everyone with her wedding gift to her loving brother and his new bride.

"Andrew, Shannon, when you return from your honeymoon, I would like you to move into the mansion on the hill, where you will call home, raise your family and be the innkeepers for the Marshall Mansion Bed and Breakfast." Everyone was speechless as she continued "You will have plenty of staff to help you run it with great efficiency. I have been secretly renovating the mansion with the aid of Mr. Claxton, architect and master builder from McDowell County. It will be the biggest bed and breakfast in Sleepy Creek and with all the extra visitors coming to our Christmas festival, we have need of another place for them to call home while they're here.

You and your family will be in the east wing, where you will have five bedrooms with their own baths, a large den and kitchen, for private meals with your family. The west and north wings will have five guest room each, making it a grand total of ten guest room, all with their own private bathroom. The south wing will have the large kitchen and pantry, a large dining room with cozy tables placed in lovely spaces, sleeping and living quarters for the permanent staff. The chefs and their helpers will prepare all three meals for anyone wishing to have their meals here, at the big mansion upon request.

I hope you will except my gift for two people I love dearly."

"Hattie, that's is the greatest gift I can think of, next to having Shannon as my wife!" Andrew hugged his sister "You are really something, kid-o! So young but so grown up and considerate!"

"That was one way to keep you here in Sleepy Creek!" Hattie returned his hug, then hugged Shannon "There's no one else I rather have living in the mansion and it will be a good living for you both,"

"I thought you might make that your home when you get older." Shannon squeezed Hattie lovingly.

"My heart is at the stone cottage, Shannon." Hattie smiled "That's where my home will always be."

Chapter 27

The year was now 2021, and Hattie Russel, at seventeen, just graduated high school with her three best friends, Jane Tanner, Amy Collins, and Bobby Fisher. The three girl friends had seen Bobby fisher off, on his way to join the navy, along with Bart Brower. For a graduation present, Hattie had purchased two first class tickets for their flight from a neighboring town. As they watched them drive away in Bobby's new car, a gift from his mother, Libby Fisher, the girls went to pack for their graduation get-away, New York City, compliments of Hattie, herself.

William Marshall had left her one of the wealthiest women in the state of North Carolina, even the entire U.S.A. and she knew she would never spend it all, and she rarely bought herself anything. She had given her daddy and grandpa Gideon a new milk barn with the best electric milking machine money could buy and the latest farm equipment, including the big John Deer tractor her daddy had always dreamed of having.

Hattie had supplied new commercial ovens for the Nettie's Cookie factory, were her Hattie's Patties were always a big hit during the holiday season. Drawing a new design for her latest cookie, Adam Russel created the William & Hattie's Dance, showing the young ten-year-old Hattie dancing on the handsome and tall William's feet. They too were an instant hit.

Hattie had included William in everything, naming all the charities she started in his honor. After all it was their money, hers and her William's. Hattie loved William Marshall the same at seventeen as she did at ten and her heart would always belong to him.

This trip to New York was one of the gifts to herself she thought she earned. Studying hard and making straight A's put her on the honor roll. Hattie had the smarts to run all her business's now, but she always took the advice from the old pros.

There was a lot to do in New York City, and the friends didn't waste a single moment doing everything on their list. Two broad way shows, the Statue of Liberty, the Empire State Building, Grand

Central Station, a ride through the park on a horse drawn carriage, which brought back beautiful memories to Hattie, riding next to her William and his very romantic kiss. After seeing many of the museums, the group went on a shopping spree, all the famous shops on fifth Avenue. As they walked along the crowded sidewalks, Hattie notice a very old antique shop and lying in the display window was an old diary, the very duplicate of her great- great Aunt Hattie's.

"Girls, I think I'll go inside this antique shop and look around." Hattie lifted the old latch on the door and smiled back at Amy and Jane "Want to come inside here? They have some really old stuff."

"I'm not into old junk, Hattie." Jane looked at Amy, who had her eye on Macy's. "Do you mind if we head up to Macy's department Store?"

"Suit yourselves, I shouldn't be long." Hattie slipped inside the dimly lit room and made her way to the display window. The sale's clerk, an older gentleman wearing wire rim glasses, approached her and ask if she needed to see something inside the display.

"The old diary, is it for sale?" she really wanted the old book and was hoping for a yes.

"That it is young lady. You've got a good eye for a real antique." The man reached in and pulled out the beautiful white diary. "It's from the early 1800's and you might be glad to know it has never been used." He held it out to Hattie "Would you care to look at it?"

"Thank you." Taking the old diary, she opened it to the first blank page. It still looked surprisingly white." Tell me sir, is there someplace I can have something engraved on the cover?"

"Now isn't that interesting!" the old gentleman's eyes twinkled with surprise "How could such a lovely young lady know this old diary is a special engraving addition, put out for the Christmas Holidays in the year" before the man could finish his statement, Hattie said softly

"1814!" She knew she had taken him by surprise again "Does it surprise you that I know the exact year, mister?"

"Mr. Welch, my dear." He smiled and shook his head "Now how would a beautiful young girl know such things about something this old? Does your family own an antique store or something?"

"No Mr. Welch, but I own my great-great aunt's diary from 1814 and it was a gift given to her with Hattie Russel engraved in gold letters on the top." Hattie put out her hand "I too am named Hattie Russel, after my aunt."

"Tell me Miss Russel, did your aunt's friend have a lot of money?" Mr. Welch pushed his glasses up on his nose "This diary sold for 100 dollars back in the 1800's, just the plain book, the graving was another fifty, seeing it was done in gold."

"My aunt's best friend gave her the diary, Mr. Welch. Her name was Pattie Marshall. Perhaps you've heard of the book, The Mystery of the Box in The Attic?"

"Of course! The book telling what happen in…Sleepy Creek, North Carolina, about the missing Marshall family!" his eyes lit up with new interest "And you are the writer, the ten-year-old girl that solved the mystery, along with the wealthy, William Franklin Marshall!"

"That's me. My William and I solved the mystery together and it cost me my one and only true love, William." She looked down at the pretty book to keep from showing her fresh tears. "I miss him every day and I want this diary to write down my happiest moments with William.

"That is very moving Miss Russel." He took the book and went to the front "To answer your question about an engraver, that would be me. I can put anything you choose to be placed on the cover, as long as it's not too many letters"

"Could you put William and Hattie, and in gold if you have it?" Hattie reached inside for her wallet "Whatever the price, I will pay it, Mr. Welch. I think I was led to this shop and your window display."

"It will be pretty pricey with the gold lettering, dear." He looked up sadly, knowing this book was very sentimental to Hattie Russel but he had to make a living. "Are you sure you want to go in debt, my dear? Credit card interest can rob your savings and you appear to be in high school."

"I graduated from high school this year, Mr. Welch and I am more than capable of paying for my purchase, with cash." Hattie smiled at his confused expression "Mr. Marshall will be buying this gift for me, he left me almost everything he had. I assure you, I can afford the price."

"Land's sake child, if that's a fact, you probably don't even know just how much you have!" with a pencil he wrote down the names, William and Hattie. "I will have it ready by noon tomorrow, if that's alright by you?"

"That will work out beautifully, Mr. Welch." Hattie paid half the bill and would give him the balance when she picked up her treasure. "I will see you at twelve, sharp! Good day, sir."

Now Hattie sat in William's comfortable arm chair and entered her first entry into William and Hattie's diary.

Saturday, December 17, 2014   Dear Diary, today I went with daddy to the market in the town square, to sale my Hattie's Pattie's. That was my first encounter with William Marshall.

Hattie went on to write down every detail of her times with her William, and at the end of each page, she would end with: "I love you my dearest William and I will forever! Hattie Russel.

Chapter 28

Hattie's sense of business kept everything in Sleepy Creeks humming right along and keeping herself busy, the years hummed by as quickly. Hattie found herself riding up to the Marshall Country Club in William's fancy carriage. Mr. Edwards was a much older man now, but Hattie kept him employed as her coachman. Like most of William's old employees, they stayed on to serve the young girl that stole their employer's heart in 2014.

The year was 2024, the two-hundred and twentieth anniversary of the founding of Sleepy Creek by William Marshall. Hattie had asked everyone coming to the dance to wear 1804 clothing, the year it was founded. As always, the big event had been sold out and everyone there was expecting their hostess to be wearing her usual new beautiful long dress.

It had been ten long years since she came to her first dance at the special Christmas Event given every year on December 23, but it was different then. Hattie still had her William and the night was magical to the young ten- year- old. William had a way of making everything special. Now, Hattie chose to go in alone, to sit in their special place with the velvet curtains she could close if she felt like crying.

Hattie had many suiters, who ask her out on dates or to dance with them at the Christmas dance, but Hattie always graciously refused. No one could ever replace her William, so she would sit alone this night with only her beautiful memories to comfort her.

Hattie had chosen to make a speech in honor of William, due to the anniversary and had ask that she might sing a song in his honor. Their song, the song he had sung in her ear on this very dance floor. She had prayed that she might get through it without crying. Hattie had a CD made with nothing but different singers performing their song "For I Only Have Eyes for You," which she would play every night in the stone cottage when she was alone. Hattie never fell to cry when she heard the music and singing. She would close her eyes and see him lowering his face to kiss her.

The MC, walked to the mic and ask everyone to have a seat, then he introduced Hattie.

"Ladies and gentlemen, it is with great honor I introduce our own Hattie Russel. This young lady has stepped in the big shoes of William Franklin Marshall and she has done a remarkable job in keeping his dream alive and Sleepy Creek flourishing! Please welcome her and do not forget to give her your best regards for a healthy-happy new year." He held out his hand and helped her on the stage.

When the applause died down, Hattie smiled out at the many familiar faces sitting around the huge dance floor.

"Thank you all for the warm welcome. The town of Sleepy Creek began as a dream from one very special man, William Franklin Marshall, who came to a little run- down place and decided to make it his home. William purchased most of the land surrounding Sleepy Creek and chose the high bluff facing the town to build his home, for his wife Susanne and their baby girl, Pattie. The year was 1804 when they came to Sleepy Creek and in 1814, the disappearance of the family occurred, when Pattie was ten, the same age I was in 2014, when I met William and fell in love.

"I want this night to be a remembrance of William Marshall, and everything he has done for our small town. He and Susanne started this Christmas dance two hundred and twenty years ago and it's been a Christmas tradition ever since. I had my very first dance here ten years ago with my William and I shall cherish that memory for the rest of my life. It was during that dance, William sang me our song and I have ask to perform it for you tonight. I know I will not sing it as wonderful as my William did, but it will be coming from my heart. I would like each of you to stay seated while I sing 'our song' for William's honor and reflect on the many ways he is still helping each of you today."

Hattie turned to the M C, and nodded for the orchestra to begin, then picked up her mic.

"Are the stars out tonight, I don't know if it's cloudy or bright, for I only have eyes for you, dear..." Hattie sang from her heart, as she closed her eyes and William's face came into view and from that moment on she was singing only to him. In her head, she could hear his voice join her in their song.

It was a long night, but Hattie finally got back home to the stone cottage. She walked to the mantle and touched his handsome face. It was her painting to him, the Marshall family painting rest on the left side of it and the painting of Aunt Hattie and Pattie, on the right. Before going to bed, Hattie would write in her diary about the day's event and end it as she did every night: "I love you William. I will love you forever. Hattie Russel.

Tomorrow would be Christmas Eve, another anniversary, ten years since her William went away and left her alone.

The town of Sleepy Creek woke up to another snow, and Hattie drove out to the Russel farm to spend another Christmas Eve with her grandmother while the family worked at the cookie factory. It was just one more tradition for Hattie. Family was always important to her, so this is where she would be the day before Christmas, reliving things Nettie and Hattie had done together during her twenty years on earth.

Nettie Russel, now eighty-years-old, still like to do the cooking for what family members still lived at home. Besides Andrew and Shannon being married, so was Peter, Philip, James, Simon and John. Matthew considered himself a lady's man, and dated many different women in town and brother Thomas, now twenty-three, decided he wanted to stay a farmer like his daddy and grandpa Gideon. So, Matthew and Thomas remained at home.

Now that her granddaughter was not around to watch after, Nettie took to watching soap operas on the television and during the holiday season, she preferred the Hallmark station with all the Christmas movies. It made her day less lonely while the family was away. But when Hattie was visiting her, she gave all her attention to her special granddaughter.

The day passed by quickly as the Russel's had their annual Christmas Eve supper then head off to church for the Christmas Eve services.

Hattie hugged her family goodnight as they left the church and promised to see them for their annual Christmas get-together. All Hattie's brothers and their wives and children would be in attendance to have Christmas dinner and then unwrap the many presents lying beautifully under the big Christmas tree, found on the Russel farm.

Hattie returned to her quiet stone cottage. All the staff had been given the holidays off to be with their family just like she had done every year. Her wealth brought her one important luxury, a special

Christmas switch, to click on all the Christmas lights at once, unlike growing up on the farm, where Hattie found herself every holiday, crawling under curtains and behind furniture to plug in individual lights. The candles in each window, the big wreath on the front door, the huge Christmas tree, the candles sitting on the fireplace mantle, and her favorite, the stable, where they place Mary, Joseph, the shepherds, the wise men, camels and sheep. A glowing angel hung magically on an almost invisible fishing wire attached to the ceiling. A special light was set up for baby Jesus to show He is the light of the world.

Hattie was glad she didn't have to plug in each candle, tree, mantle lights, or her beautiful manger scene in her new home, their beautiful home. She walked over to the fireplace and gazed into William's face in the painting. As always, tears laced her warm brown eyes.

"William darling, you have been apart from me ten years this day. It should feel like an eternity, my dearest, but it seems like only yesterday you were holding me in your arms and telling me goodbye. To keep you near, I smell your pipe, kept supplied with your favorite tobacco or your aftershave, so manly and strong.

I've come a long way since the outspoken young girl you fell in love with, my darling. When you left, I believe Hattie Russel left with you, at least a big part of me. I could never find joy in doing the things I used to do, fishing with my brothers, taking a tube ride down Sleepy Creek, swimming with my friends, or going sledding, the movies, or ice skating. My family has been so understanding, my love and they try to keep me occupied when I'm not busy running the mill or our other business. I say ours William, because it will always be yours and mine.

The Christmas dance is as beautiful as ever and I still have sherry at our private table, alone, and think about our first date. I tried to sing our song, as an honor to you my love, but I must admit, you sing it so much better. Don't think me foolish beloved, but I heard you singing with me, but only for my ears.

Our song, For I Only Have Eyes for You, makes me cry every time I play it. I had a CD made, with as many entertainers as I could find, singing our song, along with some you could sing to, if you were only here, sweetheart.

Speaking of singing, a group of carolers will be coming by

tonight to serenade me, to cheer me up for being alone. You would enjoy them William. They dress in 1800's clothing and harmonize beautifully as they sing happy, cheerful Christmas carols. I think their goal is to cheer up all shut ins and lonely people, left alone during the holidays.

I was delighted to find an old diary just like my Aunt Hattie's, so I could write all our happy moments in, starting with our first meeting in the market. To a ten-year-old, you were the most handsome, mysterious man I have ever seen. I think I fell in love with you that very afternoon, William Marshall. It saddens my heart that our time was cut short and that I shall never know what it would be like to make love to you, my darling. Now, all I have are dreams and memories with you, but they are so precious, I shall hold them in my heart for all eternity."

A soft knock came on the front door and Hattie glanced at the grandfather clock, sitting by the fireplace. The carolers were a bit early but that suited Hattie, she could turn in early. Picking up a tray of William and Hattie's cookies to hand out to the loyal group, she opened the door and the tray slipped from her hands. Hattie bent down and put the unbroken cookies back, then looked at the floor, expecting to see several pairs of boots, and her eyes grow wide when they fell on a single pair of shiny black boots.

Chapter 29

Hattie's heart began to beat faster as her eyes wondered up, from his boots to his black pants, then a long wool overcoat. Standing up on shaky legs, she stared at the tall man's back. His attention seemed to be on something down the street. Was this just a cruel joke someone was playing on her, she thought, as she watched him silently. There was something about him that made her hope, so she whispered his name

"William."

Turning slowly to face her, William Marshall smiled, as he took a deep breath. She was here, just as he had hoped and dream about. After ten years, his Hattie had grown up into a beautiful woman.

"Hattie, my darling." Came his soft words.

"William, am I dreaming? Are you a ghost or have you come to take me to heaven, my dearest love?" Hattie didn't know whether to laugh or cry, what she felt was confused joy.

"Hattie, sweetheart, you are nether dreaming or seeing a ghost, who has come to carry you to our home in heaven." William appeared to be as confused as the girl he had given his heart to ten years ago. "Hattie, my love, may I come inside by the fire? It's freezing out here."

"Oh, darling, do come in!" she laughed softly "You must be alive if you can feel the cold, but how William, I don't understand."

"I don't know how I came to be here, standing at your door." Taking off his coat, he warmed himself by the fire as he hugged Hattie.

"Darling, it's our door. This cottage has always been yours and mine, William." She held him tight, afraid if she let him go, he would vanish from her sight. "Can you remember what you were doing right before you found yourself on our door step?"

"As a matter of fact, I was having a walk with Jesus, discussing you and how much I love you. It was a walk my Lord and I took often." William looked thoughtful as he remembered the peaceful path they always took, among rows of giant roses, the colors of the rainbow. "This time it was different. There seem to be a more brilliant glow around Jesus as we walked. He would listen to my words of affection for you, dearest and there were times, He didn't speak to me outwardly but from within my soul. Before we would end each walk, he smiled at me, then disappeared, to be with one of the many people living in Heaven.

This time, instead of leaving, he stopped, and placed his hands gently on my shoulders. His face became radiant and had I not been in heaven, I would not have been able to look into such a bright light. Then Jesus spoke these words to me

"William, sweet child, live in peace and filled with faith. You will find your love. It's meant to be."

Then I found myself standing at the cottage. I made my way slowly to the door, unsure of what had just happened to me."

"William, the words of Jesus, those were the exact words he spoke to me after He took you to heaven!" Hattie felt a new sense of joy, the Lord had brought her William back home, to her. "Darling, we have been blessed by God Himself."

"Hattie, it was sad to leave my girl ten years ago and see how much it was hurting you." William pulled Hattie into his warm embrace "But I'm back now, sweet, my darling, here holding you in my arms where you belong."

"Dear William, when I opened the door and dropped my tray of cookies, thinking it was carolers coming by to sing, as they do every Christmas Eve, I was expecting to see several feet standing over me when I looked up, but when I saw your black boots, I was back at the market, ten years earlier, seeing William Marshall for the first time." Hattie ran her hand over his face, like she had done on the painting for so many years. "Only this time, you were facing out, at something down the street. Where you trying to figure out where you where?"

"I knew instantly where I was Hattie, the stone cottage at the edge of Sleepy Creek." He smiled down into her beautiful brown eyes "It's hard to forget a house you have seen off and on for over two hundred years, darling." They both laughed at the ridicules sounding statement, then he remembered the candles glowing from the cottage windows and smiling, knowing in his heart, his Hattie had to be inside. "I knocked on the door, then heard someone coming toward the cottage, so I turned around to see a small group of men and women, dressed in period clothes from the 1800's. They stopped and turned to continue down the street, as though something led them away from our cottage. I heard you say my name and my heart was suddenly alive with happiness. When I turned around, I could still see my little Hattie standing in front of me, then before my eyes, you changed into the young lady I've been waiting to marry."

"Oh William, if Christmas Eve 2014 was my most unhappy day, Christmas Eve, 2024 is the happiest day in my life!" Hattie threw her arms around his neck "The only day that can make me happier, is the day I become Mrs. William Franklin Marshall!"

"It can be our Christmas gift to each other!" William laughed with joy "Will you be my bride, Hattie Russel, tomorrow, on Christmas day?"

"Yes! Yes! Yes!" she clicked on the D.V.D. player and before she pressed the play button, she smiled.

"William, I sang our song at the Christmas dance this year, in honor of you, darling. I knew I couldn't sing it as well, but I heard you singing with me, perhaps echoes from the past, but it helped me get through without crying."

"But I was singing with you sweetheart." William ran his fingers over her lips "In heaven, there are special occasions down on earth we can witness. Happy times, such as the two-hundred and twentieth anniversary of Sleepy Creek's beginning. I watched you sitting in our special place, looking very sad and sipping on what looked like sherry. I knew you were thinking about me, after all these years. I was secretly glad there was not a man sitting next to you, perhaps that was selfish of me, but I felt like you would always belong to me, Hattie darling."

"You were right William." Hattie looked at his handsome young face "There was no room left in my heart for another darling. It was completely filled up with you."

"I could tell you were nervous about singing our song. I could read your thoughts, your great emotions the song brought out. The memories of us dancing, you first standing on my feet then I swept you up into my arms. I needed to hold you close and sing the words, only meant for you to hear." William looked down once more at Hattie's lips, luscious and full, ready to be kissed. "When you closed your eyes, I knew you could see my face and I realized I needed to join you, so you could relax, knowing your true love was there, with you."

"And here you are, my darling William, and yet you look different, younger than before."

"That's because I am younger, precious. I became thirty in heaven where all adults are close to the age of Jesus. Children can remain children, if they choose or grow up in heaven. My Pattie chose to grow up so she could be the same age as her very best friend." William looked at the painting of his daughter with her best friend.

"Aunt Hattie, of course!" Hattie laughed "I know Hattie is finally complete, she has found her dear friend Pattie."

"No, you found her dear friend Pattie. Your aunt is very proud of you, Hattie Russel." He took her into his arms "Your William is very proud of you too. You saved all of us that day. You are quite a girl, Hattie."

"William, I been waiting for ten years for you to kiss me again!" this time it was Hattie who ran her fingers over his lips "Are you going to just stare at my lips, Mr. Marshall, or are you going to kiss your girl?"

"I'm going to kiss my girl now and every day, for as long as we live!" he lowered his head and parted his lips over hers into a passionate kiss. "Hattie, my Hattie." He whispered and kissed her again.

While they continued to kiss, the player switched on, as if by an invisible hand, and it passed over the vocals, the single piano version began playing. William and Hattie looked over at the player, then back at each other. William bowed his head and took her hand.

"Could I have this dance Miss Russel?"

"I would love to dance with my handsome fiancée." Hattie put her arms around his neck and stepped up on his shoes "Now sing our song, my dearest William."

With his beautiful baritone voice, William Marshall sang their song, For I Only Have Eyes for You. As the music continued, they wrapped closer in each other's arms as Hattie spoke softly

"Are my family in for a Christmas surprise!"

"Hattie, sweetheart, we got that Christmas miracle!" William's eyes spoke volumes of love "Merry Christmas, Hattie."

"Merry Christmas, William!"

Hattie and William Marshall were married on Christmas

morning and just as Hattie had predicted, her family were happily surprised by their Christmas miracle.

The old Marshall Mansion set quietly now, the residents had gone to bed and were sleeping soundly. It was Christmas Eve after all, and Andrew and Shannon's two children knew Santa Clause would be coming down the big chimney, along with all the children staying in the inn with their parents. Santa always found the good children, wherever they lay their head.

The big house was dark, except for the electric candles lighting up the stairway. Up in the attic all appeared dark until the stroke of midnight. A light began to shine brightly in the old window but this time it was a large electric white candle, placed there by the young Hattie Russel in 2015. It was a special candle that was on a timer that was set to go off every Christmas Eve at exactly twelve o'clock It was the Christ candle, welcoming the coming of the King of Kings! The birth of our Savior, Jesus whose light shines out on the hearts of everyone who believes in Him, that they too will walk in the light!

So, the light shines in the attic on Christmas Eve and Jesus, the light of the world, shines forever, in the hearts of all His sweet children, both old and young!

The Box in the Attic

"December 25, 2024   Dear Diary, today was a most special Christmas! My Christmas dream came true and it was truly a miracle, a loving gift to me and William, by our Lord! Everyone was overjoyed with happiness for us, but kept asking, how could it happen? A man dead and taken to heaven ten years earlier, now alive! I had one simple answer for them, with God all things are possible.

Thinking back to December, 2014, I remember well the authorities retrieving the remains of everyone trapped inside the mansion for two hundred years, but there was no sign of any remains of dear William. They all assumed he had just vanished into dust and was swept away by the winter winds. You know what I think, Dear Diary, I think our Lord Jesus took William up, whole and complete, knowing His future plains for William and me. He told both me and William that it was meant to be, our love was meant to be. So, he waited until I grew up, then he joined us as one.

William and I were married this morning down at the court house, promising each other a church wedding in the near future. Mr. Sheppard, the justice of the peace was more then happy to perform the ceremony early on Christmas morning, after issuing us a marriage license. We drove straight to the farm to tell my parents and grandparents the good news, then we all went to Christmas services at church, where we gave our thanks to God for our Christmas miracle.

This afternoon, we went back to join the family in our Christmas supper and to open gifts. As always, all the family was there and we had a wonderful time.

My good friend, the old Hattie has come back! I have been only half of a person ever since I lost my dearest love, but he has returned to me. When he turned around and said my name, I could feel myself coming back alive! Praise the name of Jesus forever!

I must close now, Dear Diary. My wonderful groom will be coming inside soon from putting up the carriage and our two horses, Prince and Knight. William was so sweet and romantic wanting to hook up the carriage to take to the farm, even though I had given the coachman the holidays off. I need to go get ready for my William. At long last we can fulfill all our needs for one another. Last evening, William was such a gentleman and said he would sleep in the guest bedroom so he could have his bride completely on the wedding night. In his delightful humor, William said he had already waited for his love for two hundred and fifty years, one more night would not kill him.

The night as come Dear Diary, to make love at last! I'm happy I can go in as a virgin, to seal our blessed marriage for all eternity. It feels like I've been on a long journey, but I'm back, Hattie Russel is back. Hattie Russel Marshall